The Sage and the P

R. Wo

Book Two of T

Bramoria

This is a work of fiction. Similarities to real people, places, or events are entirely coincidental.

THE SAGE AND THE PHOENIX

First edition. November 2, 2022.

ISBN: 979-8223078647

Written by Blake R. Wolfe.

One

THE SHOCK OF THE ICY water forced the breath from Tyler's lungs as soon as he sunk below the surface. Crashing through the water from such a height felt like hitting stone. His body plunged deeper and deeper, the water crushing in around him, the sudden pressure in his ears nearly unbearable. His eyes flew open and in the flurry of bubbles he could just make out a light far above him. It seemed like an impossible distance, but he hadn't come this far to give up now. Kicking as hard as he could he fought his way back toward the surface, his lungs screaming for air. His soaked clothes and sword weighed him down, pulling him toward the bottom lost somewhere in the darkness below. Tearing at the water with every last bit of strength he had, he slowly ascended. Every passing second was agony as he fought back the urge to breathe, the light never seeming to get any closer. Just when he thought he could hold it no longer, his head finally broke the surface. Gasping he immediately began to choke and sputter, sucking in nearly as much water as air.

Around him the turbulent water crashed, waves rolling over him and pushing him back under. He fought his way back to the surface, scanning the horizon for somewhere to go. It wasn't clear if he was in a big lake, the ocean, or something in between. However, several hundred feet away he noticed trees, white sand, and tall dark cliffs thrusting into the sky. The sight gave him the faintest glimmer of hope that they wouldn't drown in the middle of whatever body of water he was in. Next to him he heard the gasps and yells of others as they surfaced, all of them struggling against the waves and wind. Turning about he could see the forms of Ninsar, Koto, and Danny struggling to stay afloat.

"Follow me!" he cried, trying to point toward the island. "There's land over there!"

Taking a second headcount to make sure everyone was there, Tyler began to drag himself through the water, paddling as hard as he could toward the landmass in the distance. The waves continued to crash over him, forcing him underwater several times. Struggling to keep his head above the surface, Tyler forced his way forward, focusing all his remaining energy on getting to the island. He was tossed back and forth the closer he got, the waves crashing over the sandbars and coral that loomed up from the darkness below him. More than once he felt his legs scrape against the corals painfully, but he didn't have time to see how badly they'd been damaged. It wasn't until he felt his feet finally touch the sandy bottom that he dared to think he might survive. Dragging himself through the shallows he eventually crawled up onto land, managing to pull himself just far enough to not be swept back in by the surf. Rolling over onto his back, he stared up at the darkening sky, the last hints of sunset giving way to stars. Somehow they'd managed to escape Clay's fury and by some miracle he wasn't dead.

Coughing caught his attention and he turned to the side. There, digging his clawed fingers into the sand was Koto. He collapsed with his head turned in Tyler's direction, his eyes shut as he panted. He'd looked bad before when they pulled him out of the dungeon, but he looked even worse now. His arm was still damaged from the Fossars and the rest of him was one giant bruise from whatever torture Clay had inflicted upon him. Koto only managed to open his eyes for a moment before he let his face fall back to the sand. Behind him was Ninsar, who somehow had enough energy to get to her feet. She was walking in Tyler's direction, but didn't stop as she passed by, her eyes flicking to him for only a second. Following her eyeline in the opposite direction he saw Danny on his hands and knees coughing up the salty seawater. He looked like he'd hit a fair number of the reefs, his pants in tatters and watered down blood staining the edges of the fabric. Ninsar kneeled down at his side, her hand patting his back to help him expel the water from his lungs. Her soft voice was drowned out by the sound of the waves.

"Get away!" Danny cried, pushing Ninsar off of him. She tumbled backward into the sand as Danny's eyes fixed on Tyler. "What have you done?!" he yelled, his face turning red with fury.

Tyler didn't know what to say. What did Danny mean? He'd saved all of them from being killed by Clay and his army of soldiers. If he hadn't gotten them out of there, they'd already be dead in a pool of their own blood.

Danny clawed his way through the sand until he reached Tyler, grabbing him by the front of his shirt and yanking him up painfully. "Why the *fuck* did you take me away?"

"He... He was gonna kill us!" Tyler shouted back, trying to pull Danny's hand from his shirt. He could feel the heat rising under his collar. "I had to get us out of there. I'm the only reason we're still alive!"

"You've doomed me to die," Danny choked, the tears of fury forming in his eyes. "He was going to *save* me, Tyler! I could have lived!" He kept trying to shake Tyler by the collar, but his movements were weak. "I don't have much time left and... and thanks to you... I'll never get any more!" His words were torn apart by sobs. "I'm going to... die now and... it's all your... fault."

Ninsar put her hands on Danny's shoulders, trying to pull him away from Tyler. He fought for a moment, then gave in, collapsing backward into her lap. Curling into a ball he buried his face against her leg, his body shaking from the sobs. She shot Tyler a venomous glare, then went back to consoling Danny.

Tyler didn't know what to say. He'd saved his friend from the one person who'd made it abundantly clear he wanted them dead, who murdered people at the drop of a hat. But somehow, even with all his brave talk and determination to accept his own mortality, Danny had given into Clay's tricks at the last minute. Tyler wanted to reach out and shake some sense into him, to tell him how stupid he was being, but even that felt childish. How could he blame him? For the past four years Danny had lived every single day with his illness, never knowing if or when it would kill him. Then, when he'd finally accepted his death, cruelty had given him hope once more only for Tyler to rip it away from him again. Part of him wondered if that had been part of Clay's plan just in case they got away. Even if it was unintentional, it worked. If Tyler couldn't make him see the truth, he was going to lose Danny like he almost had back in the walled garden.

Tyler felt a hand on his shoulder and he turned to see Koto standing behind him, sand still plastered onto one side of his face as he cradled his injured arm. His wet clothes showed how little he'd been fed in the castle dungeons and his eyes were full of the deepest exhaustion.

"Come on," he whispered, pulling on his shoulder. "Leave him be."

Reluctantly tearing himself away from Danny's sobbing form, Tyler pushed himself to his feet and followed Koto up the beach to the treeline. There they both collapsed into the seagrass, feeling a strong breeze blow over them, the smell of salt and fish fresh on the wind. For a long while they sat there in silence. Koto tilted his head back to look at the stars while Tyler kept his eyes fixed on Ninsar and Danny further down the beach. The sand almost seemed to sparkle in the moonlight, but the beauty was lost on him. There were so many emotions flowing through his mind that he could barely sense the world around him.

"So," Koto said, finally interrupting the silence. "I see you've managed to get yourself into a considerable amount of trouble in my absence."

Tyler shook his head in irritation, not wanting to play Koto's games.

"It seems your friends are a lot worse off than any of us thought," he continued. "I didn't realize you knew the king until he showed up after the dragon attack. Why didn't you tell me?"

"I didn't know he *was* the king," Tyler replied. He turned his gaze to Koto. "Did you really try to kill him?"

"No," Koto said with conviction. "I didn't. But I did try to turn him in for poisoning his father. When he called for the guards and blamed it all on me, you can guess who they believed. Especially since my blade was covered in my own father's blood."

Tyler's head hung low. "I don't know if this is the right time, but I need to know. What happened to him? Why is he like this? Nothing makes any sense."

"I came to the castle about a year ago," Koto began, his gaze fixed on the ocean in front of them. "My father was a member of the royal court and an advisor to the king. I was hired with Nikolas and Gordath to be a protector to the king and his family. Almost immediately I was assigned to Clay and we were sent off so he could train with the Sage. The prince had shown a sudden aptitude for magic and the king had a good relationship with the Sage at the time." Koto's face darkened as he recalled the memories. "But it turned out there were some things I didn't understand. After only a week the prince's powers had grown exponentially. Taken with his new abilities, he decided to steal an artifact from the Sage, killing his assistant in the process when he got caught." Koto shook his head. "I'm sorry to say I did nothing to stop him. In fact, I made sure he got back home safely, believing him that the gauntlet had gone haywire of its own accord.

"But when we arrived home his entire demeanor changed. With his new power he started to push harder and harder, trying to force the kingdom into an all out war with the Sage, claiming he was impulsive and dangerous. He fought to have his power stripped from him by the academy, citing the incident with the gauntlet as proof that the Sage had only evil intentions. After all, why would a man who claimed to be good own or create such items? I stood by listening to his claims grow larger and larger, all the while knowing that it wasn't my place to say anything. That was when I noticed my father giving the prince counsel as well."

"What happened?" Tyler asked, knowing full well how the story ended.

"Many things happened all at once. My father told me to keep my mouth shut if I wanted to live and the very next day the king fell mysteriously ill. It was barely a week before the king relinquished his crown to Clay temporarily. All the while the prince and my father bent the academy to their will, their selfish whispered plans about dragons and awakening the power of the Divinarae spelling out doom for all of Bramoria. The only thing I was sure of was that they wanted to make Clay king permanently and expand the empire while sending thousands to fight the Sage and take his power. War was the goal and they didn't care about the cost, that much was clear." Koto's ears lay flat against his head. "I'm not sure what they wanted with the Divinarae, but based on what I'd heard, I knew it couldn't be good. It would have been a runaway disaster if I hadn't intervened.

"Somehow they managed to remove the crown from the king permanently, convincing the academy to support the prince's endeavors. With their vote of confidence and the support of the queen, they were able to make it happen. The night of his coronation I followed him on a hunch, noticing his immense pleasure at being crowned the new king. I already knew things were bad, but when I saw both my father and Clay standing over the old king with blades in their hands, I couldn't stop myself from taking action. I fought them both and eventually cornered the prince. Just as I went to make the final blow, he activated his magic that had grown even more powerful than I realized. In an instant he cast a spell that switched his place with my father, my blade piercing through his ribs and into his heart." Koto paused for a long moment, his gaze empty and far away. "I barely had a moment to react before Clay was calling up the entire garrison for my arrest, claiming I'd tried to murder them all. He then killed his own father in front of me and even stabbed himself in the leg to make it look more convincing. I barely escaped with my life."

"It seems unreal that Clay could ever be capable of such things," Tyler said, hanging his head low. "Why does he think you're working with the Sage though? Is that another lie he's telling?"

"No. That one is true," Koto sighed. "I'd been passing him information anonymously for quite a while after we arrived back at the castle. I wasn't able to give him much and I'm sorry to say I withheld a lot of it, worried that I'd be found out."

Tyler shook his head, overwhelmed by the information. "Danny should hear this too. He needs to understand what kind of a monster Clay has become."

Koto nodded. "How did you find out?"

"I read the book," Tyler replied. He immediately felt a twinge of pain in his chest. "One of the servants died getting it for me."

Koto's ears perked up. "Do you still have it?"

"No," Tyler replied, shaking his head. "Even if I did have it, Clay found a way to hide portions of it so nobody could see what he's up to. The servant, Faus, was caught and killed when he tried to return it for me." He pulled his knees up to his chest, burying his face between them. "Every time I try to help, it all goes wrong. Everyone keeps getting hurt because of me. When I close my eyes all I can see is the look on his face as Clay tore his heart out..."

A hand came to rest on Tyler's shoulder and he glanced up. Koto had a sad smile on his face.

"You're the only reason I'm still alive," he replied. He pointed down the beach. "And the only reason that girl is free and your friend is safe. Give yourself some credit where credit is due. You saved us all."

"We're in the middle of nowhere with no food, no water, and we're enemies of the crown. And now, above all else, my best friend hates me." Tyler rested his forehead against his knee. "I've just made everything worse." He felt a deep ache in his chest, trying to fight back the tears that threatened at the corners of his eyes. "I should have just done what everyone wanted. If I hadn't lied to my mom, hadn't run away with my friends, none of this would have ever happened." He sunk down further, the world around him dissolving from his senses. "It's all my fault."

Two

The dawn came and Tyler found himself still awake, curled up in the grass at the edge of the island forest feeling sorry for himself. It had been two days since he'd gotten any sleep and he felt as if a strong breeze would unravel him completely. He had his knees pulled to his chest and his face toward the sea, watching the waves crash against the beach. The sound of the grinding sand had lulled him into a meditation-like state, time slipping by in the darkness of night without his noticing. But now that the sun was up, it was harder to ignore the world around him. Unable to lose himself in his thoughts any longer, he slowly got to his feet, not bothering to dust away the sand stuck to every inch of his body. A quick glance showed the others to still be asleep, his gaze resting on Danny and Ninsar cuddled against one another for a moment. There was a twinge of jealousy in the pit of his stomach, his brows furrowing together. Shaking his head he trudged down the beach and headed for a rocky outcropping, hoping to get away from everyone before they woke up. The last thing he wanted to do was talk to any of them. At least not yet.

The night had given him a lot of time to feel bad for himself and the situation he now found himself in. His mother was still back at the castle with no idea who he was, lost in some dastardly spell. He kept wondering if he'd just told her the truth about college, maybe he could have avoided everything that had gone wrong. Not only that, but inviting Clay along had obviously been a stupid mistake. Actually, the more he thought about it, being friends with Clay seemed to be the biggest mistake he'd ever made. Sure, his home life was terrible and his father was an alcoholic and an abuser, but Tyler had seen all the other red flags Clay displayed and chose to ignore them. For years the guy had been getting further and further into trouble, his sense of morality growing more ambiguous more with each passing day. It seemed that being sucked into Bramoria was the final straw that tipped him over the edge, giving him the chance to finally act on the base impulses that Tyler had suspected existed all along. Stealing the book had been Clay's idea and Tyler would never forgive him for it. Every bad thing that had happened in the past few weeks was made possible by his insatiable need for trouble.

But it all came back to Tyler. If he'd not invited Clay, maybe they'd still be back home and maybe he could have talked Danny into going back on his chemo. It was too late for that now and in the end he knew he had nobody to blame but himself.

Between his bouts of self pity he found moments to wonder about what they should do next as he climbed the rocky outcropping and found a place to sit amongst the sun baked seaweed and gull droppings. The waves crashed around him, cold salty sea spray flecking across his skin. He knew they had to find the Sage, that much was obvious, but he had no idea where to even begin looking. Koto had mentioned the old wizard liked to wander, however, he hoped Koto could give them some sort of direction. If Clay had once visited him, then he had to have a home somewhere that hopefully stayed in one place. Tyler thought back to movies he'd seen and hoped the wizard's home didn't have legs or a sassy sentient fireplace.

There was one thing working in his favor and that was the Sage had obviously been keeping an eye on him. He'd visited during the dragon attack to save them and to meet face to face with Tyler when they teleported to the capital city. Tyler reached into his pocket and drew out the amber colored mage stone that he'd used to transport them across the world the night before. He wondered if he could use it to contact the Sage once more.

Holding the stone in both hands and closing his eyes, Tyler began to concentrate on it, trying to find the familiar electric feeling of the magic inside it once again. At first he could just barely feel the tingling in his fingers, the sensation hardly more than static. Forcing his thought and will upon the stone, he searched for more. Suddenly the power grew and surged through his hands like lightning. Tyler nearly threw the stone out of fright, fumbling it at the last moment until he got a hold of it once again. Gripping it tighter he concentrated on his intention, willing it into the stone. He wanted to speak with the Sage, to call him to their location so they could get this nonsense over with. He hated Bramoria and it was time to go home. Even if his friends never forgave him for it, it was what needed to be done. As the magic swelled around him he closed his eyes, waiting for the moment the Sage would appear in front of him at last.

Instead of the wizard appearing on the rocky sea stones like he'd hoped, Tyler felt himself sucked backward into the darkness of his mind. It was a similar feeling to the teleportation, but less jarring and painful. He opened his eyes to find himself still sitting, but now in the middle of a vast starscape like he had been the first time the Sage spoke to him directly. Galaxies and nebulas swirled around him, the starlight shining from all directions. He couldn't see the surface he was sitting on, only felt its solidity under his butt. Glancing down he noticed the mage stone was glowing brightly in his hands, the magic obviously activated and swirling in the air around him. He wondered how long it would last.

"So," a familiar deep voice said from behind him. "You wish to speak with me."

Tyler looked over his shoulder, a man standing behind him in a billowing hooded cloak. He held the same gnarled wooden staff with a sapphire blue gem set into the top, a misty energy flowing around it. Immediately he felt a sense of distrust but there was no one else to turn to now. All other avenues had been closed to him.

"Yes... I... I need your help," Tyler managed to say. "I'm ready to go home."

He couldn't see the man's face under the hood, just the barest bit of jaw and hints of gray peppered stubble.

"And you wish for me to send you there?"

"With my friends, yeah," Tyler replied. "You've seen what this place is doing to them. I have to get them out of here." He lowered his head back toward the ground. "Especially Danny. He needs to see his parents before he..."

The Sage waited for him to finish, but Tyler said no more. He took a few steps, his staff creating a hollow echo as it struck the invisible floor. Instead of answering Tyler's please, the wizard asked another question. "Did you read the book?"

"Yeah," Tyler nodded.

"And you learned something?"

"Unfortunately."

The Sage waited a moment longer. "And what did you learn?"

Tyler sighed. "That Clay is a monster. He's been manipulating everyone into doing his dirty work. He killed his own father, he's taken over the academy, he kidnapped my mother, and I don't even know all of it, not since he figured out a way to hide sections of the book." Tyler lifted his gaze back to the Sage. "I should have gotten rid of him years ago. He's a terrible person and I've been ignoring the signs for a long time."

The man stopped, his hooded face turning toward Tyler. "Absolutely astounding," he huffed, tapping the staff impatiently. "You had the book in your hands, read it cover to cover, and yet you are more blind now than ever." He lifted the staff and used it to lift Tyler's chin. "You have so much more to learn, yet you refuse to open your eyes."

"No," Tyler spat. " I don't need to learn shit. Me and my friends need to go home so we can get back to our lives. Danny is going to die here if we don't get out soon!"

"Your friend will die either way," he replied casually. "That is a certainty. Especially if you don't stop ignoring the obvious."

Tyler could feel the rage building up in his chest. "And what about Clay?! You're just going to let him continue *killing* people?"

"Why do you care?" the Sage asked, tilting his head to the side. "You don't even believe this world is real."

"Of course it's not real! It's a fucking book!" Tyler pushed himself to his feet. "Shit like this doesn't exist in real life!"

"Hundreds of worlds exist on your bookshelves and you visit them often whenever you're in need or want to escape. You've lived those stories over and over, lived the lives of heroes. Did they not help you? Provide you with the adventures and escape you were searching for? Does that make them less real than the things you see outside your window?" He pointed to the healed cuts on Tyler's arms and the wound on his face from where Clay had struck him. "Are those not real enough for you? Have you not been changed by this place? What is *real* in your mind?"

"Will you just get me the fuck out of here you piece of shit?!" Tyler yelled, no longer able to contain his fury. "Are you some sick fuck getting enjoyment out of this? This isn't a goddamn book! People are getting hurt and dying here!"

"I thought you said none of this was real? Why would you care who dies here if they are only figments of your imagination? How can a fake world hurt you?"

Tyler opened his mouth to retort, but nothing came out. The Sage was right, if Bramoria was fake, why did he care that its people were dying? It looked real, but then again, so did movies and games. Instead he stood there with his fists balled at his sides and his teeth clenched, pissed off that he didn't know what to say.

"You have much to learn Tyler Wilson. Nobody ends up in Bramoria by accident, there is always a reason, a lesson that must be learned."

"So you're not going to help me," Tyler huffed. "You're just going to sit there and teach me a fucking lesson?"

"I didn't say that." The man took a step back, his staff striking the ground at his side and giving off blue sparks. "But maybe if you spend a bit more time here, you'll begin to understand what Bramoria is trying to teach you. Find your way to me and we can talk. Maybe you'll find something along the way to clear your mind or something to help your friend. After all, there are many kinds of magic in Bramoria that can help the sick and the dying."

"What should I look for?" Tyler was on the verge of pleading. "I want to save Danny, but I don't know how!"

"Bring to me what you've learned on your journey and when you reach my crystalline palace, I'll help you and your friends fix what's been broken." Mist began to swirl around the hooded figure as the stars blinked out one by one. "And remember, the book's price is collected regardless of the method of acquisition. Just because it was stolen doesn't mean it didn't cost your friend something."

"How do you know that?" Tyler turned his head, trying to get a better look at the face under the cloak. "Who are you?"

"I'm the Sage, I know everything."

The mist swirling around the figure suddenly burst into bright blue flames and in an instant he was gone. Tyler stood in the starlit void, the galaxies around him fading away, as he tried to piece together what the Sage had told him. It seemed there would be no help from anyone, at least not until he did something in return. Once again Tyler had to put in a lot of work to please others while the only thing he really wanted to do was disappear. He was more confused than ever about Bramoria, Clay, and the Sage.

Glancing down at the slowly fading mage stone in his hand he realized he didn't really have a choice as usual. If he wanted to save Danny or his mom, he had to go to the Sage for help, even if it meant walking across the entirety of Bramoria on foot. He just hoped Danny would be able to survive the journey.

Tyler closed his eyes as the void around him went dark. The next moment he opened them to find himself back on the rocky outcropping, the sea splashing around him and the calls of the gulls overhead. The mage stone was still clutched in his hand and for half a moment he had the thought to throw it into the ocean. A voice sounded behind him, pulling the thought from his mind.

"Couldn't sleep?" Koto came up beside Tyler and took a seat on the hard stone, trying to avoid a small puddle forming in a weather worn pocket. He waited silently for a moment, his arms crossed over his knees. "It's really pretty out here."

"It's trash just like everything else in this world," Tyler scoffed, shoving the stone back in his pocket. "I'm so tired of this fucking place."

"Did something happen?" Koto asked, his mangled ear tipping to the side.

"Yeah," Tyler huffed. "I called the Sage for help. Fat fucking lot of good that did."

Koto's eyes grew wide. "He was here?"

"No. I called him with the stone." Tyler wrapped his arms around his legs. "He's not going to help anyway, at least not right now."

The surprise faded from Koto's face. "What did he say?"

"Some stupid wizard shit about how I'd learned nothing from Bramoria and now I need to find my way to him on my own. Apparently he doesn't want to help me until I can help him or something." Tyler gritted his teeth. "Fucking dumbass jedi bullshit."

"Did he say what you needed to learn?" Koto leaned a bit closer. "Maybe if you can figure out what he wants, he'll send you home."

"Why the fuck should I have to figure out what *he* wants?" Tyler snapped, the emotions rushing out of him in a sudden burst. "What about what *I* want, huh? Why does nobody ever give a fuck about that? Clay and Danny only care about themselves and my mother wants to live vicariously through my accomplishments, but not a single fucking one of them stopped to ask what I want out of life! They just take, take, take!" Tyler wanted to scream. "And I just keep giving because I don't know what else to do..."

Koto reached out a hand, placing it gently on Tyler's back. "What *do* you want?" he asked softly.

"I don't know," Tyler replied, shaking his head. "I don't want my friends to die... I don't want to be here... I just want to live my own life without having to answer to anyone. That's all I've ever wanted. I'm tired of everyone dictating my decisions before I can make them." He looked back up at Koto. "But I don't know what I should do... I didn't even want to leave home. Running off with Danny and Clay was the only thing I ever did by myself and look where it got me." He could feel the tears threatening at the corners of his eyes. "Nobody gives a shit about me or what I think."

"I do," Koto said, patting him on the shoulder. "And I'm here to help you if you want it. It's the least I can do for getting me out of that dungeon." He pushed himself to his feet and held out a hand to Tyler. "And because I *want* to help you."

Tyler stared at his hand. "Why?"

Koto shrugged. "I figure we're friends by now, aren't we? Isn't that what friends do?"

"Not in my experience..."

"Well," Koto said, leaning forward and taking his hand before pulling him to his feet. "Then let's change your experience." He looked up to the sky, shielding his eyes from the sun and pointing off to the northwest. "The Sage's palace is nestled in the valley of the Dravin Peaks beyond the Blightwood Forest." He turned back to Tyler. "I'll help you get there."

"What if that's not where I want to go?" Tyler asked, testing how Koto would respond.

"Then we'll go another way. This is *your* journey," Koto said, poking a finger into his sternum. "You lead the way and I'll be your guide."

Tyler turned back over his shoulder, glancing down the beach and to the woods where he could just make out the shapes of Danny and Ninsar lying in the grass. "We have to help Danny," he sighed. "And the Sage seems like the best choice. He said he could help him."

"I agree. If we meet any other healers along the way, it won't hurt to ask."

"Okay," Tyler nodded. He reached up and wiped his face on the back of his sleeve. "Thanks, Koto."

"No problem," he replied, taking a step forward. "Now let's go try to talk some sense into your friend. Hopefully he's calmed down a bit since last night."

Tyler felt anxiety flare in his chest, but nodded anyway. "Alright."

Three

Tyler sat on the grass with Koto at his side. Danny was lying on his back opposite with his head in Ninsar's lap, looking up at the blue sky above. He was doing everything he could not to make eye contact with Tyler. It was clear from his body language he was still furious about losing his imaginary chance at being cured by Clay. As much as Tyler wanted to shake him and make him understand that it had all been a ploy to gain his allegiance, he stayed quiet. Instead he let Koto do the talking, he was better at it anyway and the only one among them unlikely to have an emotional outburst. He'd spent the past half hour telling Danny everything he knew about Clay and his past, although it seemed to have done little to shift his mood.

"The Sage's palace resides to the northwest in the Dravin Peaks, that much we know," Koto said, pointing off in the distance. "However, we have no idea where we are or if there's a way off this island. That's the first order of business." He glanced over to Tyler. "Now that at least two of you have an awakened mage stone, we should be able to find some way out of here without too much issue." Pushing himself to his feet, he pointed over to Ninsar and Danny. "You two stay here and comb the beach. See what you can find and gather driftwood for a fire." He turned to Tyler. "And you're coming with me. We're going to find some food. I'm sure all of us could use a good meal and a day's rest before we start wandering off into the wild unknown."

There were grunts of acknowledgment from the other two as Tyler got to his feet. Stealing a quick glance at Danny, he saw the look of disgust before he quickly turned away. Feeling the irritation prickle over his skin, Tyler followed Koto into the trees in search of their breakfast. They were only a few yards into the woods before the breeze was almost completely cut off and the oppressive humidity of the understory became so thick it felt hard to breathe. Beams of light broke through the canopy, illuminating small patches of forest floor and the brown leaves that lay there unmoving. Koto was a few feet ahead, his ears swiveling on the sides of his head as he listened to their surroundings. Birds sang in the trees while small lizards scampered about in the leaf litter chasing flies. Tyler doubted Koto could hear anything of use over the cacophony of nature around them.

"Any idea how we're going to get out of here?" Tyler asked, breaking the silence at last. "Or where we are?"

"I should be asking you that," Koto replied. "You're the one who cast the spell. Where did you take us?"

"I don't know anything about Bramoria," Tyler said, shaking his head. He already felt stupid for using such magic, but there had been no other way out at the time. "I was thinking about a safe and secluded place, somewhere far away from the castle and Clay. It made me think of the giant lakes back home and the dunes surrounding them, so I guess it took me to the next best place."

"Well," Koto said, looking up at the canopy. "I guess I should be thankful we didn't end up in the middle of the ocean then. That would have been bad for all of us."

"I'm sorry..."

"Don't be," Koto said, waving him off with a smile. "You did the best you could at the time. Nobody else could have gotten us out of there except you. If you hadn't, we'd all be in a dungeon right now and probably at least two of us would be dead, if not more. That was an incredible piece of magic you pulled off for your first spell. I'm sure it caught the king quite off guard."

Tyler still felt guilty as he kicked at the dried leaves, disturbing a couple green lizards in the process. He supposed Koto was right, that he did keep them all from Clay's murderous grasp, but now they were stranded with nowhere to go. If Clay and his mages were as powerful as everyone claimed, they could be tracking them at that very moment.

"Could Clay find us here?" Tyler asked, speaking his thoughts aloud. "And send the academy after us?"

"Simple magic can be used to find somebody, yes, but it's limited. Usually you can only see the person and their surroundings for a few feet. Unless you recognize where they are, it can be hard to pinpoint a location," Koto said, nodding his head. "But getting to them is much more difficult. The mages are more than capable of teleporting *back* to circles they've already created." He glanced back at Tyler. "But trying to leap to a new place is dangerous, as you well know now. It can have very unexpected results like appearing high in the air, underwater, or even underground."

"Underground?"

"Those mages are typically never heard from again. I imagine their bones are nothing but dust within a few moments from the pressure of the stone." Koto sighed. "That's why I'm not worried about them finding us here. Although, if Clay uses the Divinarae, he could spy on us and see what we're up to as often as he wants to. If we cross a place where his mages have a circle already created, that could give him a chance to get the jump on us. Thankfully there are very few in existence and only in the largest cities."

"So we're safe here?"

"For now."

"Koto?"

"Yeah?"

"I read something weird about the Divinarae in Clay's book... something that didn't make sense to me."

Koto stopped, turning back around. "What was it?"

"Well, a lot of it had been wiped away, so I wasn't able to really make out what was going on." He looked up at Koto. "Can it be used for other things besides divining the future or spying on people?"

One ear cocked to the side. "I'm not sure." He lifted a hand to his chin, his head tilted toward the ground. "I was told it was created centuries ago by a group of powerful mages. By combining all their power and pouring it into an ancient pool over decades, they were able to create something nobody had ever seen before. However, it took all their power to make it and in the end they all died before they could explain what it was. At least that's the story I was told, although I'm not sure how much truth there is in it.

"The academy claims there were papers left behind and they've studied the pool ever since. But the only thing I've heard of it doing is seeing the future or finding lost things." He glanced back up at Tyler. "The pool itself is made up of raw magic in liquid form. It's possible it could do other things, but so far nobody has figured out how to harness its power." He cocked his head to the side. "Why? What did you read?"

Tyler hesitated for a moment, trying to figure out how to put what he'd seen into words. "There was something about the dragons and the Divinarae. Like the two were linked somehow. But like I said, there were a lot of pieces missing."

"It's definitely interesting," Koto nodded. "And a bit worrisome if I'm being honest. Clay already unearthed the Divinarae for himself and the academy, which doesn't bode well. With the power of the grimoire, there's no telling what he might have discovered."

"Things really never get any easier do they?"

Koto gave him a small smile. "Life is complicated, but I'm sure once we reach the Sage, we'll be able to get some answers. He has been around for at least a millennia after all."

"How is that even possible? Is he a lich or something?"

A serious expression crossed Koto's face. "I hope not. That would probably spell disaster for all of us. I'm surprised you've heard of them."

"Oh, so you know what a lich is, but you've never heard of a phone?"

Koto shrugged. "I guess." He turned back toward the path and ushered for Tyler to follow, pointing to a clearing up ahead. "Let's go see what's up there. Maybe we can figure out where you dropped us and plan our way out."

Tyler nodded and followed behind as Koto picked up the pace. Ahead he could see the dark edge of the forest falling away into bright open air. He thought he could hear the sound of waves once more even though they hadn't been walking for very long. Tyler had assumed they were on an island that must be smaller than they originally thought. Most of all he hoped they'd find a way off of it. The likelihood of a ship sailing past anytime soon seemed slim and it wasn't like they could just write a message in the sand and wait for a plane to pass over like they did in old tv shows. Unfortunately all those years of watching *Gilligan's Island* as a kid had left him wholly unprepared for life on a deserted island if that's where they really were. He had a feeling his own adventure would end less in wholesome comedy and more in starvation if they weren't careful.

At the edge of the forest Koto came to an abrupt halt, causing Tyler to run into him. He opened his mouth to apologize, but the sight in front of him made the breath catch in his throat.

"Whoa..."

The scene that spread out before Tyler was like a tropical dream. He and Koto stood at the top of eroded black rocks some twenty feet above the water. A turquoise sea lapped against the white sand beach lining the island. A handful of dark stones dotted the water, jutting their sharp edges above the surface in places. Between them schools of fish swam, their bright scales catching the sunlight. Pops of color erupted in long lines between the stones, Tyler recognizing them from the coral structures he'd seen in his biology textbooks, all manner of pinks, whites, and reds. Gulls flew overhead, their cries filling the air as they searched for fish straying too close to the surface. A cool breeze blew from the sea, washing away the stifling humidity of the forest they'd been traveling through and cooling their sweat soaked skin. Not far away another island of black cliffs and trees rose out of the sea, then another beyond that. Tyler's gaze followed a long chain of them led into the distance until they finally met a larger piece of hazy land on the horizon. He'd never seen anything so beautiful in his entire life.

"This... This is amazing," he said, his eyes scanning the breathtaking scene. "It reminds me of back home... but bigger."

"It's been a long time since I saw the ocean," Koto sighed, the wind ruffling his hair. "Too long."

"Did you grow up near it?"

"My father spent most of his time in the king's court, but the house and land he owned was on the edge of the sea." His eyes grew distant as he stared out at the horizon. "Veordya aren't looked up with much kindness, so my father wanted to keep me and my mother out of the public eye. I spent most of my youth there until she died."

"I'm sorry."

He shook his head, glancing back to Tyler. "Don't be. It was a long time ago." Koto sighed. "After that I went to a training school for a couple of years before I was hired on at the castle as a bodyguard."

Tyler cocked his head to the side. "Huh. For some reason I thought you were a lot older than me."

"I'm just nineteen."

"I think I might have turned eighteen in the past few days, but I've lost track."

Koto smiled. "Happy birthday."

Tyler opened his mouth to respond, but his ears perked up as he caught something strange in the breeze. Koto's ears twitched as well, swiveling in the direction of the beach. It was music of some kind, but unlike anything Tyler had ever heard before. The melody was soft and low, like a lullaby, seeping into his senses and washing away his cares. In less than a moment, Tyler forgot all about home and his problems, lost in the faint melody drifting on the wind.

"Come on," he said, leaning over the edge. "I want to go take a look."

Koto glanced at him, a dreamy look in his eyes. "Okay," he replied without hesitation.

Forgetting all about the exhaustion threatening to swallow him whole, Tyler threw his legs over the side of the rocks and began to climb down. He felt more energized than he had in days. Koto was right beside him, his injured arm no longer hindering him. The song seemed to grow as they descended, the tune now recognizably a voice. Tyler wondered who could be on the island with them and why they would be singing. He hadn't seen a boat and it seemed unlikely that people lived there, but then again the voice couldn't be mistaken. He wondered if it could be sailors. They liked to sing. And that would mean a boat was nearby. His curiosity piqued, he kicked off the dark stone and dropped the last few feet into the sand. With a satisfying crunch Koto landed next to him and both of them turned back to the water searching for the source of the sound.

Tyler was the first to step up to the edge of the water, the waves washing over his boots although he barely noticed. The singing had grown louder, but for some reason he still couldn't figure out where it was coming from. He stepped a little further in, the cool water flowing over the tops of his boots and filling them to the brim. For some reason he knew deep in his gut that he had to find the voice, it was all he could think about. He knew that if he found it, all his cares and worries would disappear. Everyone would be saved, including Danny, and all his wildest dreams would come true. It was a powerful feeling and one he couldn't ignore.

Koto looked to be similarly attracted, keeping pace with him as they both waded their way further in, the water already up to their waists. Scanning over the surface Tyler spotted something, a dark shape moving quickly across the sandy bottom. Suddenly another came up next to it, both of them swimming fast in their direction, spiraling around one another. Something deep in the back of his brain told him to get to shore, but the voice ringing in his ears commanded him to stay. There he stood, watching the ominous silhouettes draw closer and closer.

They darted around the edge of a black stone sticking up out of the water. For a moment they disappeared, but as Tyler kept his gaze fixed in that direction he watched as a woman appeared from the other side of the rock. She was completely naked, her nearly purple skin glistening in the sun as dark black hair streamed down her back. Beside her a male figure joined her. He was similarly nude, but his hair was a lighter brown and his skin a pale gray complexion with striped patterns on his arms and shoulders. His heart beat faster. They were gorgeous and he felt a deep surge of desire in his belly, commanding him to walk forward. Both of them leaned on their elbows, propping themselves up on the rock in seductive poses. Tyler watched as they opened their mouths and began to sing the same song that he was hearing on the breeze. In a flash he felt his focus crystalize and he began to walk toward them, the water quickly rising to his chest and lapping against his neck.

Four

Tyler couldn't take his eyes off the strange people on the rocks in front of him. Even as he began to paddle, his feet no longer touching the bottom, he fought to keep his head above water so he wouldn't have to break his gaze. They were exceptionally beautiful, probably the most beautiful people he'd ever seen. Something about them was so deeply alluring, but he couldn't figure out what it was. Instead of thinking about it too much, he just kept swimming, trying to reach them as fast as possible. Koto, however, turned out to be the faster swimmer despite his injured arm and reached the rock a few feet ahead of him. Pulling himself easily out of the water he took a seat on the stone between the singing pair, their hands immediately reaching up and stroking his face and chest.

Immediately, Tyler felt a burning jealousy erupt in his belly. He clawed his way up the rock, nearly unable to pull himself up thanks to the exhaustion plaguing his limbs. At the top he was met by a pair of warm smiles, the singers reaching out and helping him further up so he could join them. Their skin was cold and clammy, but for some reason he found it comforting, the coolness of their touch soothing under the hot sun. Upon closer inspection he found their bodies covered in a series of strange patterns, almost like scales. Their forearms had a small fin on the underside and under their ribs were sets of gills. All of it seemed perfectly normal with the song filling his ears. Even when he noticed their torsos didn't end in legs, but in a long curving body like that of a shark, he didn't think twice. Nothing seemed off about the situation in the slightest.

It wasn't until the male reached forward and ran a hand across his face that he felt a sharp shock from his pocket, pulling him to his senses. He looked down and saw the mage stone outlined against his leg, the amber light glowing through the fabric. For a moment he was still mesmerized by their song, but as the male reached forward again he felt another sharp sting from the stone. All at once his thoughts and fears came flooding back. He glanced over and saw Koto and the female locked in an embrace, their lips pressed together. Her arms were behind his back, sharp black claws puncturing his skin. Thick red blood stained his clothing, but he didn't seem to notice. A hot streak of pain filled his own body as the male reached forward and grabbed the back of his head, his claws piercing the skin as he pulled him closer. Fear flooded his system as he realized what they were, myths of sailors drawn to their deaths filling his head.

The male leaned closer, the song once again filling his ears. Without a moment to spare, he reached down to his belt and ripped his dagger free. Before the siren knew what was happening, Tyler jammed the blade into his side, the metal slipping easily through the gills on his ribs.

Cold blood oozed across his hand as a furious screeching unlike anything Tyler had ever heard split the air, nearly tearing his eardrums in the process. The female ripped herself away from Koto, her face dripping in blood from where she'd already been chewing on his companion. She cried out and lunged at Tyler, her claws slicing through his clothing, leaving bloody gashes behind. Crying out, he toppled backward off the rock and splashed into the water, the dagger slipping from his grip.

"Koto!" Tyler yelled as he resurfaced, choking on the water that was slowly turning red around him. "Help!"

A splash from the other side of the stone signaled the sirens leaving their dazed prey behind. Tyler knew he had only seconds to get out of their reach. He threw his arms up on the rock, pulling with all his might to get himself out of the water. His muscles strained and another streak of pain shot through his body as he felt a cold clawed hand wrap around his ankle.

"Koto!"

The shift from song to screams seemed to shake Koto from his daze. He lifted his hand to his face, his fingers coming away bloody from his torn lip. His gaze drifted lazily to Tyler, his eyes growing wide just before Tyler felt himself tugged off the stone and under the surface. He hadn't had time to take a breath before he was yanked to the bottom, the sirens swirling around him. Teeth claws came at him from all directions, the movements so fast they were dizzying. Tyler tried to kick and punch as they came near, but nothing seemed to connect. He felt several new wounds open up on his body, the salt water stinging viciously as the water around him darkened.

His eyes caught a glint of metal several feet away resting on the sandy bottom, but as he reached for the dagger a hand took his ankle, then another took his wrist. They were twisted cruelly as he was pulled back, now face to face with the sirens. Underwater their beautiful visages faded away revealing a pair of monsters that looked more like sharks than anything. The striped patterns on their skin became more pronounced and the mouths opened too wide, displaying rows of sharp teeth. There was an emotionless hunger in their black eyes that made Tyler's blood run cold. As they pulled him closer he shut his eyes, knowing there was nothing he could do to stop them.

Screams of agony filled the water around him as his eyes flashed open once more. A dark cloud of blackish blood welled up from the female siren in front of him. The shifting sunlight of the waves caught a long blade sticking out through her chest. She reached down, her claws clutched around it as if trying to pull it free and undo the damage. As it was ripped out she slowly coiled in on herself like a snake and began to sink, the water growing dark around her. Behind her was Koto floating in the water, his shortsword grasped in his off hand.

The male siren let go of Tyler instantly and rushed for Koto, ramming him at full force. The sword was knocked from his hands as he was slammed against the stone, air bubbles escaping his mouth. Tyler fought his way back to the surface, his lungs burning from being under for so long. Using the stone to thrust himself upward he gasped in a breath of fresh air and immediately dove down once more. Kicking as hard as he could until he hit the bottom, scooping up the sword. To his left the female siren had stopped moving, her body floating lifelessly in the current. To his right however, the male was bashing Koto against the rocks over and over again. Koto tried to fight back, but the siren was too strong. Tyler watched his eyes roll back as the last of the bubbles escaped his lips, blood staining the water around him from the multiple lacerations he'd received.

Knowing he had only seconds, Tyler kicked off the bottom, rocketing toward the siren with the blade held aloft. He intended to run him through like Koto had the female, but the siren saw him coming. At the last second he dodged out of the way, the blade only piercing through his shoulder. Another ear splitting scream filled the water as the male cried out, tearing himself free of the blade. He looked up at Tyler, clutching the wounded arm in his claws. His head turned to the female, obviously dead, sinking to the bottom as her body slowly filled with water. With one last venomous glare, the siren hissed and shot off in the opposite direction, a trail of dark blood marking his path.

Tyler didn't waste any time. He let the sword fall from his grasp as he grabbed Koto's lifeless body and pulled him toward the surface. Gasping for air, he pulled Koto around to a partially submerged section of the stone. Ignoring the pain from his wounds, he clambered up onto the stone before dragging Koto up behind him. Leaning his ear down he checked to see if the man was still breathing. But there was nothing.

"Fuck fuck fuck..." Tyler whispered, looking to shore then back to Koto. There was nobody to help him. "Okay. I can do this," he said to himself, pulling Koto's mouth open. "They do it in the movies all the time. It can't be that hard, right?"

Reaching down he pinched Koto's nose shut, took a deep breath, and pushed their mouths together, exhaling into his body. To his surprise Koto's chest rose and he let go of his nose. Placing both his hands on the man's chest he counted ten compressions, hoping it would be enough but having no idea how many he should do. Leaning down again, he blew another breath into Koto's body. Halfway through he felt the man under him convulse and he pulled back, water spouting from Koto's mouth. Grabbing his shoulders, he turned the man on his side, hoping to make it easier for him to expel the water from his lungs.

"By the gods..." he wheezed, coughing and sputtering as he clutched his chest. "I hate... water..."

Tyler had to laugh at the irony, the stress of the whole situation too much to bear. "You didn't tell me there were murderous mermaids here." He flopped down on the stone beside Koto. "That would have been good to know."

"I... didn't know..." Koto huffed, coughing once more. "I've never... seen anything like that... in my life." He took a moment to catch his breath, coughing between them to get the water out. "What... What were they?"

"Those were sirens," Tyler explained, staring up into the blue sky as he tried to ignore the pain coursing through his body. "They draw you in with their songs, then they drown you and eat you."

"How... How do you know that?"

"I've heard stories about them in my world."

Koto paused for a moment, taking a few deep breaths. "Maybe you're not the only one that's been to Bramoria then."

Tyler turned his head toward him, lifting an eyebrow. "Are you trying to say that those stories are from other people who traveled here?"

"Maybe."

He looked back up at the sky. "Are there unicorns here too? Sea monsters? Giant white whales?"

"Nobody's seen the white whale in a few decades," Koto said. He rolled over to his stomach and coughed a few more times. "But the unicorns are so thick in the north that they're almost considered a nuisance. As for sea monsters, those *sirens* aren't the only thing haunting the oceans, you can be sure of that."

"Wonderful," Tyler sighed as he pointed across the water. "I'm so glad we're going to have to swim to get to the other island. Hopefully they don't try to eat us again."

"We'll find a way." Koto looked back at the island they'd come from. "But first we need to get back on land and find some food and water. I've drunk enough sea water to kill a man." He leaned over the side of the stone, staring down into the water. "And I dropped my sword."

"I'll get it back," Tyler said, crawling his way over to the edge. "You just get yourself back to land." He glanced down at the wounds covering both their bodies. "Can you make it?"

Koto gave him a stiff nod. "I'll wait till you come back up and we'll go together." He paused for a moment, lifting his gaze to Tyler's. "Thanks for saving me."

"You saved me. I should be the one doing the thanking." Tyler reached in his pocket and pulled out the amber mage stone once more. "Besides, it was this thing that shocked me. We'd both be dead if it hadn't reacted. I wonder if it knew I was in trouble."

"I've never heard of one acting of its own accord before," Koto said, eyeing it suspiciously. "What could that mean?"

Tyler shrugged, slipping it back in his pocket. "Not a fuckin' clue." He pulled himself to the edge of the stone, the water lapping against his chest. "I'll be right back."

With that Tyler slipped off the stone and dove into the clear turquoise water once more. The sting of the salt had faded somewhat as he opened his eyes again. Diving down to the bottom he searched along the sand. He found the sword easily and returned it to Koto before he dove once more, looking for the dagger that he'd dropped. A few minutes later, after several dives, he found it wedged in between two boulders resting atop a piece of pink coral. The shine of the steel reflected the color around it making it almost impossible to see. As he slipped it back into his belt he saw the body of the female siren resting on the bottom, her limp body swaying back and forth in the current.

Surfacing for one more breath, he dove down to get a better look. A large gash tore through the center of her chest, the blood having washed away from her exposed flesh and bones. Already there were several of the reef's fish picking at the wound, helping themselves to an easy meal. He pulled his eyes away, the sight making his stomach turn. Scanning over her he found nothing except for a small rope tied about her waist. For a moment he thought to ignore it, but something told him to take a closer look. Pulling the small knot apart it came free and he pushed off the bottom, heading back to the surface. As he grabbed the edge of the stone and hefted the rope up, he saw a small pouch attached to it.

"What's that?"

"I don't know," Tyler replied. "I just thought we could use the rope for a raft or something." He coiled it up on the stone. "It was around the siren's waist."

Koto leaned forward and pulled the pouch toward him, undoing the drawstring slowly. He pulled it open, holding it out so Tyler could see what was inside. To his surprise it was completely empty.

"Hmm," Koto hummed, shrugging his shoulders. "Why would she keep an empty pouch?"

Tyler reached out and took it. "Maybe she collects shells or something?" He reached inside, checking the interior for sand or hidden items in the seams. However, instead of feeling the fabric around his fingers, he felt cold air as they slipped in further than they should have gone. "What the hell?" He pushed his arm down to the elbow, his gaze lifted up at Koto as his arm disappeared. "I can't feel anything."

"A bag of boundlessness," he whispered, his eyes growing wide.

"That," Tyler said, staring at him intensely, "is the dumbest name for a bottomless magic bag I've ever heard."

Koto ignored him. "I wonder what's in it..."

"Once we get to the beach, we'll find out," Tyler replied, tying it around his arm with the rope.

"How?"

"It's easy. We just turn it inside out." Tyler glanced up, a small smirk on his face. "*Everyone* knows that's how you empty them."

Five

It took a fair bit of time to get back to the other side of the island with their new wounds. Not only that, but they had to stop several times to pick the fruit they found along the way, trying to carry as much as they could. Tyler dropped several of them into the siren's bag, but carried some as well, just in case they were unable to retrieve them. During their search they were also lucky enough to find a small pool at the base of the stone cliffs that allowed them to fill their waterskins. Nearly an hour later they found themselves flopping down in the grass where Danny and Ninsar had managed to gather a fair amount of driftwood for a fire. However, as soon as they appeared, the questions started.

"What the hell happened to you?" Ninsar asked, her mouth hanging open as she stared at the two bloody men in front of her. "You both look like you were mauled by bears!"

Danny looked up at the pair of them, his eyes glancing over them, but he said nothing.

"Close," Tyler chuckled. "Apparently there are sirens here." He looked at Danny. "Killer mermaids."

"What?!" Ninsar gasped, her hand going to her mouth. She looked back at Danny. "We were just in the water trying to catch fish! We could have died!" Her eyes narrowed at Tyler. "Why didn't you tell us sooner?!"

Tyler held up his arms, gesturing to his body covered in wounds. "We were a little busy if you didn't notice," he sniped. "Besides, we killed one of them anyway. Or well, Koto did."

"Thank you, Koto," Ninsar said, turning away from Tyler. "I knew you would prove yourself to be useful." She glanced back at Tyler. "Unlike some."

"Look," Tyler huffed, growing tired of her constant displeasure with him. "I know I accidentally got your friend killed, but you don't need to be such a bitch."

Ninsar's hand went to her belt, but Danny was faster. His sword flashed out, leveled at Tyler's throat in an instant. His face was beet red and his eyes full of fury. Tyler glanced at the blade, then up at Danny. No matter how hard he tried, he couldn't form words to express the betrayal he felt.

"Okay," Koto said, reaching out and pulling the blade away from Tyler. "Everyone needs to calm down. There's been enough bloodshed for one day." He gently moved Danny back to Ninsar's side, getting him to take a seat in the sand. "We've all been through a lot and we now know there's danger all around us. This is not the time to start fighting amongst ourselves." He pointed a finger at Ninsar. "We're going to need to work together if we want to get out of this. Okay? There's no need to pick unnecessary fights."

She let out a long sigh. "Fine." Her eyes flicked back up to Koto. "So what's the plan?"

"We're working on that," he replied, going back to his own spot near Tyler. "There's a chain of islands we can hop, but we'll have to be careful. If the sirens come back, we won't stand a chance against them." He looked at Tyler. "Their songs can be very... alluring."

"We could try to fashion a raft and paddle our way over," she suggested.

"We have no tools or supplies to make such a thing." Koto hung his head. "Although if we stayed here long enough, we could make it all ourselves." His gaze shifted to Danny. "But I know we're on a tight schedule."

"You mean I won't live that long," Danny said flatly, his glare still fixed on Tyler. "Because *someone* decided to not give me a choice."

"Oh yeah," Tyler snapped. "I'm really sorry I didn't let Clay kill us all and feed you a bunch of bullshit lies!"

"You don't fucking know he was lying!" Danny yelled back. "He has the entire academy under his thumb and more magic than *you'll* ever have! We have no idea what he could have done!"

Koto lifted a hand, cutting them both off. "That's enough!" he cried, getting back to his feet. "Tyler did what he thought was right and from what I've seen of your so-called friend, I agree he would have said anything to get the chance to kill us all." He pointed a finger down at Danny. "We're going to get you some help but we are not your enemies and neither is Tyler." His ears went flat against his head. "Stop being a selfish brat for half a fucking seconnd and use that brain between your ears!"

Danny opened his mouth to retort, but snapped it shut. Without a word he pushed himself up from the sand and stomped off in the opposite direction, headed down the beach.

"Tiragan!" Ninsar called, getting to her feet.

"Leave him," Koto commanded. "Let him walk it off. He needs some time to come to his senses."

Tyler watched him go for a moment before turning to Ninsar. "Why do you call him by that stupid name?" he hissed.

"Because he asked me to," she replied, spitting venom right back at him. "Because that's who he *is*."

"Pfft. No he's not." Tyler crossed his arms, looking back toward the water. "He's Danny Johannsen. That's who he's always been and that's who he'll always be."

"Shows what little you know," she scoffed. "And how little you care. So much for being *best friends*."

"Enough," Koto roared, getting fed up with the both of them. "I've heard enough of your bickering! We need to plan, not fight."

Tyler and Ninsar glared at one another for a long moment, neither of them blinking. Koto took a seat once more and handed a piece of orange fruit to them both.

"Eat. It'll help. We're too tired, hurt, and hungry to keep doing this."

Ninsar took the soft orange fruit and turned toward the sea, her teeth sinking into it. Tyler did the same, but kept his gaze fixed on the beach, watching Danny walk further and further away. A sigh came from Koto as he bit into his own meal, realizing that neither of them were going to back down. The tension was thick in the air, the pressure of the ticking clock pressing down on all of them as they ate.

It wasn't until some time later that the sun forced them to retreat further into the trees and they finally began to speak once more. For nearly an hour they went over several different plans to leave the island that included all manner of inventions and lucky chances. However, without tools, supplies, or the promise of a passing ship, they eventually returned to the idea of swimming. With the stones dotting the water they could swim for short bursts, then rest. It wouldn't be unreasonable to hop to a new island each day until they finally reached land. However, even though it was their fastest option, it would still take them a week or more to make it to the continent and Danny was running out of time. But no matter how they tried to find a way around it, they were going to lose precious time on the journey either way.

"We'll have to swim, there's no other choice," Ninsar finally sighed. "But we'll need to be careful. Tiragan isn't doing as well as he pretends."

"What's wrong with him?" Koto asked, looking at Tyler. "I know you said he was ill and he might not recover, but is there anything we can do to help?"

Tyler shook his head. "No. Even the doctors back in our world gave up on him. They said nothing they could do would help."

"But what is it?"

Both Ninsar and Koto stared at Tyler, waiting for him to explain. "I... I don't like talking about it." Their expressions didn't change and he sighed, knowing he'd have to say it out loud. "His... blood is attacking him, from the inside. Not only that, but the illness is slowly spreading to all his organs and his skin. There is no cure for it in our world. The only thing people can do is pump their bodies full of poison and hope that kills it, but it doesn't always work." Tyler let his gaze fall away from the other two. "He's been fighting it for over four years now and now he's barely eighteen. It seems like his life is over before it even gets a chance to begin."

"That's terrible," Koto said, shaking his head.

Ninsar sat close by with her hand over her mouth, tears forming in her eyes. Despite what Tyler thought of her, it was clear she cared for Danny more than just as a palace courtesan. Something had happened between them and he felt a small twinge of jealousy in the pit of his stomach at the thought.

"Before we got pulled into Bramoria I talked him into running away with me and Clay for one last summer together." Tyler shrugged, glancing back at Koto. "I don't know what I was thinking, but Danny knew he was going to die so I wanted to try to make his last days good ones. But all I did was fuck everything up and get us trapped here."

"You were trying to be a good friend," Koto said.

"I was trying to be less of a shitty friend," Tyler retorted. "For the last six months I've ignored him, too caught up in my own life to spend any time with him and all the while he was facing the end of his own. I'm an asshole." He pulled his knees up to his chest. "It's been hard watching him struggle for the past four years and I just needed a break... it was getting to be too much to handle. Between that and my mom forcing me to fulfill her dreams for me, I just had too much on my plate." Tilting his head down he rested it on his knee. "But even that feels like a pathetic excuse. The truth is I'm too scared to face reality, too scared to face my mom, and too scared to be best friends with a person who is dying in front of my very eyes." He took a deep breath, trying to keep the tears back. "I'm a coward."

"No you're not," Koto said, placing a hand on his arm.

"Then why do I feel so shitty?"

"Because life can be that way sometimes," he replied. "And because you're doing everything you can to avoid the hard things in your life. Facing your problems is scary, but running from them is a never ending cycle that will leave you exhausted and broken. Take it from me." He paused for a moment, his gaze dropping to the sand. "Everyone has problems, but it's better to stand and meet them instead of watching your back for the rest of your life, hoping they'll never find you. Because they will eventually. They always do."

"He's right," Ninsar said, breaking her silence.

Tyler lifted his head to look at her. Her eyes were bloodshot and there were streaks where tears had fallen down her face. The expression she wore wasn't one of annoyance or hatred like before, but one of empathy and understanding.

"Tiragan needs you now more than ever," she said. "And you need him too. He doesn't want to walk into death alone and it's clear you don't want to let him do that either." She reached forward and placed a hand on Tyler's knee. "Go to him. Be a friend to him like you both want so desperately." Her mouth twisted into a sad smile. "It's going to be painful, but at least you won't regret anything when he's gone."

"There's got to be a way to save him right?" Tyler was doing everything he could to keep his tears back. "Won't the Sage help? Should we let Clay know where we are? Maybe he wasn't lying."

"Clay was lying," Koto said with finality. "Healing magic is not something he ever cared to learn and those at the academy seek power, not the ability to help others. I can't think of a group of magicians *less* suited to help your friend." He paused for a moment, his eyes fixed on Tyler. "But the Sage might be able to help. We just have to get there first."

Tyler reached into his pocket and pulled out the mage stone. "Can we use this? I can try to teleport us again."

"That could kill us all," he replied, shaking his head. "It's a miracle we survived the first time."

Tyler's hand fell to the magical pouch the siren had been carrying. "What about this? Maybe there's something in it we can use."

"I'm not sure what a siren would have that could be useful," Koto replied, shrugging his shoulders. "But maybe there's something." He looked up at Tyler. "You said you knew how to empty it?"

"Yeah." Tyler pushed himself to his feet, wiping his face with the back of his sleeves. "All the games I've played say you just have to turn it inside out."

"Games?" Ninsar said, quirking an eyebrow. "This isn't a *game*."

"You'd be surprised how much this world has in common with the games in my world." Tyler fixed his eyes on her. "I know you and I don't get along, but I'm not being foolish. I promise."

She crossed her arms, returning to her usual self. "Okay. Fine. Turn it inside out then."

Tyler undid the drawstring and pulled the pouch wide, flipping it over. He tried to push the bottom through, but he met a solid resistance that wouldn't give no matter how hard he pushed. Ninsar clicked her tongue, but Tyler ignored her, flipping the bag upright again. Pulling it open again, he slipped half his arm inside the bag up to the elbow. Ninsar's eyes grew wide and he smiled, the satisfaction of seeing her proven wrong making him feel momentarily better. Pushing his arm deeper he reached all around, trying to find the bottom of the bag so he could pull it out, but all he could feel was cold moist air. He was nearly up to his shoulder by the time he said something.

"I don't know if I can," he said, looking at Koto. "I can't feel anything."

"Maybe it's not like your *games*," Ninsar sniped, her surprise already faded.

"There might be another way to empty it," Koto replied, gesturing for Tyler to hand it over.

He began to pull his arm back out but he felt something cold and slimy wrap around his wrist inside the bag.

"What the fuck?!" he cried, trying to yank it back out, but whatever had a hold of him didn't loosen its grip. "Something's got me!"

Both Koto and Ninsar got to their feet, blades already drawn. But before they could get to him there was a violent yank and Tyler felt himself pulled toward the bag. To his horror he watched the pouch grow to accommodate his shoulder, his neck, and then his head. He was being dragged into it.

"Koto!" he yelled inside the hollow space, trying to fight his way free.

Before he could get another word out he felt another pull and the bag began to swallow him whole. Just before he slipped completely inside a pair of hands wrapped around his ankles, trying to stop his falling. But whatever had a hold of him was too strong. With one last vicious jerk he felt his feet come free and he fell into darkness.

Six

Tyler struck a hard stone surface in the darkness, knocking the breath from his body. There was a thin layer of freezing cold water that immediately soaked into his clothing, the shock from the temperature making it harder to force air back into his lungs.

"You are not my captor," a deep feminine voice said in a thick guttural accent, the sound echoing all around him. "But maybe you are food. It has been a while since she fed me."

Tyler lifted his gaze slowly, two giant red orbs alighting in the darkness, a dark round pupil the size of his head centered in each. They lifted from the ground, up and up until they towered over him, easily ten feet above him. Whatever the creature was, it was massive.

"I'm... not food," he managed to gasp out, pushing himself back from whatever was staring at him. "I promise!"

"A likely story," the eyes replied. "All food says the same thing, just not all food can talk. Usually it comes to me already dead... and partially eaten."

Tyler strained his eyes in the dark, trying to figure out where he was. He turned his head up to the ceiling for a moment, noticing a small beam of light high above them. It had to be the opening to the pouch. A shadow passed over it and he could hear voices too far away to make out. However, it was so out of reach that he had no idea how he'd ever find his way to it. The massive red eyes drew closer, hovering over him in the darkness.

"Wait," he said, knowing he had to buy himself some time. "Who are you?"

"My name is Celindra," she replied. "Although it will matter little in a moment."

"How did you get in here?" He reached down to his pocket, feeling the mage stone still tucked safely there. His fingers ran along his belt, tracing over the sheathed dagger. "What happened to you?"

"Why do you ask?" She took another step closer, the eyes leaning down so close to Tyler he could see his own reflection in their depths. "You are food. What difference does it make?"

"What if I can get you out of here?" he asked, hoping to stop her from swallowing him whole. He had no doubt a creature of that size could. "Were you trapped here by the siren?"

"Yes," she grumbled, her voice deep and gravelly. "A long time ago, when I was still barely more than a tadpole."

"I'm going to give us some light so we can talk," Tyler said, reaching into his pocket and producing the amber stone that was lightly glowing. "Maybe I can help you instead of being food."

One of the large red eyes drew so close to him that he could see the veins running through the iris. "I give you one chance," she replied. "If you don't get me out, you become food."

Tyler swallowed hard. He knew he had no other choice. "Okay. That seems... fair."

Holding the mage stone in front of him he shut his eyes, concentrating on it for a moment. When he opened them again the dim glow had grown into the equivalent of torchlight. He was surprised how easily the magic had come, even if it was a small spell. It made him think that greater magic might be possible, like the teleportation spell, if he just kept practicing. Maybe he could even learn enough to save Danny.

A small shudder ran down his spine as he looked up. In front of him, illuminated by the light, was a monstrous frog easily ten feet tall. She was wrapped in spare bits of cloth and rope, what looked to be old sails from a sunken ship. Her skin was a combination of blues, greens, and whites. At the ends of her fingers were large suckers, probably what she'd used to pull him into the bag with. However, the wide face and bulbous red eyes were what set Tyler on edge. He'd seen frogs with a similar look before, but to have one look so alien and human at the same time was unnerving. Not only that, but as she spoke he realized her mouth was in fact wide enough to easily swallow him whole like he'd feared.

"So. What do you want to know," she said, her voice low and rumbling. "Let's make this quick. It's been some time since I've had a decent meal."

Tyler swallowed hard and glanced back up at the point of light in the ceiling, hoping someone would save him. "How did you get trapped here?"

"I told you. That *bitch* tricked me," she sighed, slumping into herself. "I was a youngling like you, living in the jungle we called home. I had my own pond and all the bugs a Zaba could ask for. Life was good." A scowl crossed her face, pulling at the corners of her massive mouth. "But one day I heard a strange and beautiful song, so I followed it to the sandy shores. Before I knew it I was trapped here, locked in darkness and cold forever." She reached back and picked up a handful of fish bones from nearby. "These stinking fish!" she cried, throwing them into the darkness where they clattered across the stone floor. "This is no food for a Zaba!"

"Why does she keep you here?"

Celindra's eyes refocused on him. "Why does anyone steal a Zaba?"

Tyler shook his head. "I... I don't know. I'm not from Bramoria."

Her eyes narrowed. "Zaba make medicine. Everybody knows that."

"You *make* medicine?"

Celindra reached up with her left hand and massaged a bumpy section of her head. As she did, a thick white fluid oozed out. Tyler winced as he watched. It looked like the world's grossest pimple, but a lot slimier. Long tendrils of it stuck to her hand like melted cheese as she pulled it away. He had to stifle a gag.

"Good medicine," she said, rubbing the fluid between her suckered fingers. "But sought after by many people in Bramoria. Especially the mages."

"But why keep you here?"

The frog sighed. "I thought she would sell me, but she hasn't yet." She glanced up at the beam of light in the ceiling. "I think she's keeping me as a pet."

Tyler felt a pang of guilt in his chest. He felt bad that Celindra had been trapped there for so long, possibly years, but he was going to have to trick her if he was ever to escape. The pouch had barely been large enough to accommodate him, there was no way she would be able to crawl out of it herself. Since he didn't know how to empty it, she'd have to stay behind, at least for now. However, he'd have to convince her to help. He knew he wouldn't be able to reach the top alone.

"I wasn't lying when I said I killed the siren," Tyler said, trying to keep his voice as genuine as possible. "You are no longer her prisoner."

"How can I be sure?"

"Tyler?!" a voice called from above, the beam of light blocked out. "Are you in there?"

"There's your proof," he said, pointing up to the ceiling. "If I hadn't killed her, my friends wouldn't be just outside waiting for me."

Her eyes ran over him, searching for any hint of a lie. "You are going to let me out?"

"I have no reason to keep you here," he said, shrugging his shoulders. "But I can't get up there without your help."

Celindra pushed herself up, taking a few steps toward him. She reached down and snatched up his mage stone in a flash, tucking it under one of the ropes holding her clothing on. "Then I keep this," she said, a toothless smile widening on her face. "Just to make sure you aren't lying."

Tyler nodded, trying not to show how much he hated it. "Okay. That's fair." Slowly he got back to his feet. Glancing up to the ceiling he could see Koto's clawed hand reaching through the air, searching for him. "Can you lift me up there?"

She nodded, reaching down and wrapping her large hand around his waist. Before she lifted him to the ceiling she pulled him close to her face. Tyler could see the sticky oozing fluid on top of her head where she'd pressed it out. A stench of something putrid he'd never smelled before assailed his nostrils. It took everything he had not to vomit.

"If you don't keep your word," she said, lifting her free hand and wiping some of the white ooze across the exposed part of his chest. "Then you'll die like the liar you are."

Immediately his skin started to go numb. "What?! What is this?"

"Good medicine," she replied, her smile wider than ever. "And good poison without my help."

Before he could say anything more she lifted him high into the air to Koto's outstretched hand. Reaching out their fingers connected.

"Tyler?" Koto called, his voice hollow and far away. "Grab my arm!"

Ignoring the numbness spreading over his chest, Tyler wrapped his fingers around Koto's forearm and held on tightly. He felt himself being pulled upward as the opening to the pouch grew wider.

"I'll be waiting," the Zaba said ominously from below as she let him go. With a deep chuckle she added, "Don't take too long."

The pouch pulled wider and Tyler felt himself yanked upward. Gravity shifted strangely as he exited, the bag lying on its side in the sand. Koto dragged him out until his entire body was free, the sand sticking to all his newly wet clothes and the white sticky substance on his chest. He looked up at Koto, still feeling ill from the terrible smell that had washed over him from the Zaba. Glancing back at the bag he watched it shrink back to its normal size. The entire experience reminded him far too much of the rhino scene in *Ace Ventura*.

"Thanks," he said, lying back on the sand. He took a deep breath of the salty air. "That was awful."

"What the hell happened?" Koto asked, kneeling down at his side. "Where did you go?"

"There's a whole cave in there," Tyler replied, barely believing the words coming out of his mouth. "And a giant frog. She almost ate me."

Koto's eyes grew wide. "A giant frog?"

"Yeah. Green skin, red eyes, the whole shebang." Tyler reached up and tried to wipe the white goo of his chest. "I think she said this might be poison. Good thing it didn't get in any cuts."

Grabbing him by the wrist, Koto leaned back and hauled him to his feet. "That's Zaba toxin!" he urged, dragging him toward the ocean. "You need to wash it off *right now*!"

Before Tyler even got a chance to retort, Koto nearly threw him into the waves. He was thrown off balance as he hit the water and fell backward, the sea swallowing him up immediately. Sitting up and gasping for air he glared back at Koto who still wore a worried expression on his face.

"Wash it off!" he cried before Tyler could say anything. "Now!"

"Give me a warning next time," he growled. "What the fuck..."

Tyler rolled over and pushed himself into deeper water, trying to scrub away the sticky substance that was making his skin more numb by the second. It wasn't an altogether unpleasant feeling, but he didn't understand the cause for concern. The open wounds he had from the siren were mostly located on his arms and back, nowhere near the poison. They all stung and burned from the salt water, but he ignored them, doing as he was instructed.

He supposed the Zaba had been a bit ruthless at the end, trying to poison him to keep him true to his word. However, as he scrubbed the last of the toxin away, he felt confident her threat had been in vain. He had actually wanted to let her out, but now that she'd tried to kill him, he wasn't so sure he could trust her. She still had his mage stone though and that could prove problematic. His plan had been to keep practicing magic so he could try to help Danny or find a way home on his own. Hopefully Danny would help them for now if they came across a need for magic. Unless another dragon came out of nowhere, which seemed highly unlikely since they were nowhere near a city, they should be fine.

Trudging back to the beach, he planted his feet firmly in the sand. "There!" he yelled, pointing at his chest. "Clean enough for you?"

Koto stood staring at him as Ninsar walked up. She placed a hand over her mouth as she stared at Tyler. Both of them looked horrified. He didn't understand what their expressions were about until he looked down at his chest. His eyes fell on an intense spider web of nearly black veins streaking over his skin. What little bit of hair that had been there before was now gone and his skin felt unsettlingly rubbery as he poked at it. Following the veins he pushed his shirt aside revealing a small cut left behind by his fight with the siren. It had turned a harsh purple color, although he felt no pain at all. He looked back up at Koto and Ninsar, knowing what they were thinking. The toxin had gotten into his bloodstream, the Zaba making good on her threat. And the clock was ticking.

Seven

"What do I do?" Tyler said as he fought his way back through the surf and stepped on shore, having tried to wash it off again without any progress. "Do you have something that can stop it from spreading?"

Koto shook his head. "There's no way to cure Zaba toxin without magic or help from a Zaba themself." He glanced back at the pouch held in his hand. "Do you have your mage stone? That could be a way to get rid of it."

"No. She took it from me." Tyler could feel the anxiety welling up in his chest. "She said I had to let her out of the bag if I wanted to live, but I don't know how." He reached back and pulled the dagger off his belt. "Let's just cut it open."

"Don't!" Koto cried, snatching the pouch away from him. "If this is a bag of boundlessness, the space inside will collapse the moment you damage it and the magic will be broken. You'll never see that Zaba or your mage stone again."

"Then how do we get her out?!" Tyler waved the dagger through the air. "She's like ten fucking feet tall! I barely fit, there's no way she's going to."

"I don't know," Koto replied. "But we'll try everything we can." He glanced back at Tyler's chest. "That's only going to get worse if we don't get her out of there."

Tyler slipped the dagger back into his belt. "Fine. Everyone grab an edge and pull. I'd like to live to see tomorrow."

Undoing the drawstring once more, Koto pulled the bag open and held it out. Each of them wrapped their fingers around the edge of the fabric and took a step backward. The bag immediately began to stretch, larger than it had to accommodate Tyler's body. For a brief moment it looked as if the simplest plan would work, but as they reached nearly two feet in diameter, the tension on the fabric grew taut and it stopped moving altogther.

For a moment Tyler stared into the void, knowing it wouldn't be big enough for Celindra to crawl through. A soft bubbling growl came from within as a suckered hand reached out, wrapping its fingers over the edge. Tyler leaned back, pulling with all his weight to stretch the bag further. Another hand came out and all of them could feel the weight as the creature tried to pull herself free, one red eye pressed up against the edge of the void, staring out at the sunlight nearly within her grasp.

For a moment he thought it would work, but then he heard the popping of threads at the seam of the bag. Remembering what Koto said, he let his edge go immediately along with Ninsar, the pouch suddenly shrinking down and pinching Celindra's hands in the process. There was a cry of rage from within as she yanked her suckered fingers back in and the eye disappeared. Koto stood there holding the pouch, staring down at the beginnings of a torn seam, the fabric frayed at the edges. It was clear from the look on his face that they'd barely managed to avoid destroying it.

Tyler grabbed the edge of the bag once more and leaned over it, calling into the darkness. "Celindra! The bag is too small to get you out!"

Another cry of rage from within and the crashing of stones.

"If you give me my mage stone, we can try to get you out that way."

A deep hiss came up from the void. "No freedom, no stone! That was our deal!"

"I can't help you if you don't give me the stone," Tyler called back. "There's no other way to get you out alive."

"I know the tricks of mages," she growled up at him. "Until I'm free, the stone is mine!"

"Then I can take you to someone who might be able to help." Tyler looked up at Koto. "Maybe the Sage can get her out?"

"I'm sure he could, but it's far away." Koto's eyes glanced down at the spiderweb of black veins clawing their way across Tyler's chest. "We don't have enough time."

Tyler already knew the answer, but he had to try. "Can you remove this toxin?" he called back into the pouch. "We need more time to get to those who can help you."

A deep bellowing laugh echoed back up to them. "I am no fool, mage," Celindra sneered. "I suggest you make good on your promise within a week or you'll be food once more, if not for me then for the worms and the birds."

He looked back up at Koto, a sinking feeling in the pit of his stomach. "What do we do?"

"We ask your friend for help," he replied, pulling the pouch shut once more. "And we pray."

FOR WHAT SEEMED LIKE the hundredth time since stepping foot in Bramoria, Tyler was facing his own mortality. It was becoming a habit that he was neither fond of nor eager to keep repeating, and yet it continued to happen. The irony wasn't lost on him that his only chance for survival was the Sage and the only way he could contact him was with the mage stone Celindra had taken from him. As he trudged through the sand he wondered if Danny would be able to remove the toxin from his body and give them a bit more time to reach him. However, the harsh fact remained that at least one of them would die before they could make it to the Sage, if not both.

It struck Tyler as poetically macabre that he and Danny both had something flowing through their veins that intended to kill them. Even if the means had been cast upon them differently, their fates were the same. Both of them would die within a short time if they didn't figure something out. It was with that in mind that Tyler approached his friend who now hated him in the hopes of changing his mind.

Danny hadn't been hard to find. It seemed he'd walked down the beach for a while before finding a shady spot to sit under near the treeline. There he sat taking bites out of a bright orange fruit, similar to those Koto had found on their way back after the sirens. Tyler stopped for a moment, shaking his head. He couldn't believe so much had happened in a single day. Less than twenty four hours ago they'd been in Clay's castle with their lives on the line. Now they had teleported across the continent, gotten attacked by sirens, been poisoned by a giant frog, and their lives were once again in danger. Tyler held up his hand to shield his eyes, looking toward the sun beginning to set in the western sky. In reality, not much had changed. They'd just gone from one bad situation to another.

But maybe there was some hope. If Danny could do something about the toxin, maybe he'd be able to think of something to help him in return. Tyler took a deep breath to steady his nerves. After Danny's blow up he didn't really want to speak to him so soon, but now that he had no choice with so much on the line, he found himself anxious. Somehow he had to make Danny see that he'd been trying to help him by getting them away from Clay.

A streak of anger shot through his chest at the thought of his old friend. If not for Clay, everything would be fine. In fact, they might have already found a way out of Bramoria for good and back home where they belonged. He knew Danny wanted to stay, but he needed to understand that Bramoria was killing him. At least back home there were doctors and medicine to prolong his life if only he'd stop being too foolhardy to take it. Maybe they'd even found a new treatment for him and his parents were just waiting by their phones to give him the good news. Tyler knew it was unlikely, but he stuffed that thought into the furthest reaches of his mind. Danny had given up on their world too quickly and it was time Tyler made him realize what he'd done. He didn't care what the doctors thought, he wasn't ready to give up.

Taking one last deep breath, Tyler headed for the edge of the trees where Danny sat. The sound of his boots crunching against the sand caught Danny's attention. Tyler lifted a hand, but Danny ignored him, turning his gaze away and taking a furious bite out of the fruit he held. Feeling himself deflate a bit, Tyler continued up until he was standing next to his best friend.

"Mind if I sit with you?" he asked, pointing to the grass.

"I'd rather you didn't," Danny replied.

"Danny, I don't want to fight..."

"My name isn't Danny," he snapped, throwing the fruit into the trees. "It's Tiragan."

Tyler paused for a moment, trying to stop himself from lashing out. "Why do you insist on using a made up name?" he asked, keeping his voice gentle. "What's the point?"

Danny glared at him for a long moment. "Because it's who I am now." He gave Tyler a once over. "Not that you'd understand. All you want to do is go back home and give up the first interesting thing that's ever happened to you. You just want to be plain old boring Tyler forever."

"Well I'm sorry that you've given up on your life," Tyler retorted, his attempt to keep his emotions in check short lived. "Sorry if I don't understand why you want to just let yourself die in some strange world as a different person than you've always been." His gaze locked with Danny's. "Is that what this whole name thing is about? Why do you want to stay in Bramoria? What are you trying to accomplish?"

"I'm trying to fucking *live*, Tyler!" Danny shouted at him. "You know as well as I do that I don't have jack fucking shit for time left!" He held up the backs of his hands. "Look at me! I'm covered in more spots than I've ever been and my entire fucking body hurts! I feel sick all the time and tired... I've been feeling that way for months. Long before we ended up here." Danny sighed, slumping forward. "I just wanted a chance to have an adventure before I died. Now that I'm finally having one, I don't want it to end."

"And you're willing to just run off with Clay because of that?"

Danny lifted his head, his eyes burrowing into Tyler's soul. "Yes."

"I don't understand how you could do that..."

"How much would you pay to stay alive?" Danny asked, a serious expression crossing his face. "Ten dollars? A thousand? One million?"

"Yeah... I guess? What's your point?"

"You can't ask someone what they would pay or what they would do to stay alive, because the answer is always the same." He turned back toward the horizon. "Anything. Even if you know it's wrong." He was quiet for a long moment. "I know what Clay has done is wrong, I'm not stupid. But what other option do I have but to accept his aid?"

"You could let us take you to the Sage. Maybe he can help."

"Tyler... I'm already in bad shape. If he's more than two weeks away, I don't think I'll make it. I may be able to walk right now, but that's not going to last long as this sickness starts to eat my body away. I've seen those people in the oncology unit, they all look like skeletons towards the end."

Taking a seat beside Danny, Tyler reached out and took his hand. "Look, we're going to figure it out, alright? Maybe if the Sage can't help, he can send us home so we can get you back on chemo."

"I would rather die," Danny sighed. "You don't know what it's like to have poison coursing through your body all day long. Besides, the doctors already told me it isn't going to help anyway."

"I might have a little bit of an idea what it's like," Tyler replied, pulling his shirt aside to reveal the dark purple wound and the spider web of black veins.

"What the fuck happened?" Danny asked, his eyes growing wide.

"You remember those sirens? Well one of them had a bag with a giant frog inside of it. She stole my mage stone and poisoned me in the process." He pulled the shirt back in place. "The frog said I've got about a week to either free her or die."

Danny gripped his hand harder, his attitude shifting instantly. "What do we need to do?"

"That's what I came to you for. I need you to either set her free from the bag or remove the toxin using your mage stone. I don't care which, but we have to... I would like it if you tried."

There was a battle going on behind Danny's eyes as Tyler delivered the news. It was clear a part of him wanted to help, but a darker side flared up behind it, possibly one that felt justified that Tyler finally understood what he was going through thanks to his current situation. For a moment he seemed to struggle with what to say next, but as the tension released from his shoulders, Tyler knew what he was about to say.

"I'll do what I can to help," he said, reaching down into his pocket and pulling out his mage stone. "I don't have a lot of strength left, but I'll try. For you."

Tyler reached forward and pulled Danny into a hug. "I promise I'm going to help you, alright? We'll make it to the Sage or die trying. Together."

"One of those options seems a lot more likely."

"So what's with this name?" Tyler asked, giving him one last squeeze. He wanted to talk about anything else. "Why Tiragan?"

"It's the name of one of my favorite book characters," Danny replied, glancing down at the sand. "I used it at first because I didn't know where I was or what was going on when I woke up in that bandit hideout. But after a while, it grew on me." A smile crept across his face as he spoke. "The longer I was here, the more I realized I could finally be whoever I wanted. Instead of the Danny Johannsen that felt like he had to be the perfect little sick rich boy like his parents wanted, I was free to be whoever I desired. So I chose to be my favorite adventurer because that's who I've *always* been, I was just too afraid to disappoint everyone." He glanced back up at Tyler. "I've spent so long trying to fulfill everyone's expectations instead of living my own life and now, when I've got almost none of it left, I finally realized my mistake." His eyes grew glossy as he reached up a hand to wipe the half formed tears away. "Pretty dumb, huh?"

"It doesn't sound dumb," Tyler replied, the situation sounding all too familiar.

In that moment he wanted to come clean, to tell Danny about his life and how he didn't want to live up to expectations anymore either, but it didn't seem like the right time. That moment was about Danny, not himself. It could wait.

"Sorry," Danny laughed. "Been feeling a lot of things lately."

"Don't be sorry. Just know that I'm here for you and we're going to figure this out." He turned to look out at the horizon as the last of the sun sunk below the sea. "And we'll do it without Clay."

"How are we going to save him?"

Tyler glanced back at him. "I... I don't know..." he replied honestly. "My only plan so far was to force him back home so he couldn't do any more damage here."

"How would you do that?"

"I was going to ask the Sage."

Danny was silent for a long moment. "Do you think he can?"

"Koto seems to think so. If he's half as powerful as everyone claims, it shouldn't be difficult to get us all back home." He glanced over to Danny. "And maybe help you out too."

"Yeah..." Danny sighed, his tone unconvinced. "I suppose we can try."

A few minutes of quiet passed between them as the last traces of gold faded from the clouds and the sky took on a bluer hue. Stars began to pop into existence one by one as they stared up into the heavens. Tyler wanted to save Danny more than anything and now that they seemed to both be on the same side again, he felt a small spark of hope ignite inside of him once more. Maybe it was possible they could both make it out of Bramoria alive. He glanced over at his best friend. With a sword strapped to his back and leather armor, he looked almost like all those adventurers they'd read about as children. For a moment he forgot Danny was sick and remembered the young boy full of life and imagination as they ran around the yard looking for dragons to slay in the hedges. It was a fond memory, but one now tainted by the reality of what came after. Tyler looked back to the sky, a new resolve in his heart. If they didn't make it out, he at least wanted to treat Danny like the hero he wanted to be so badly.

"So *Tiragan*," Tyler said, pushing himself to his feet. He held out a hand. "Shall we go back and make the others know we didn't kill each other?"

Danny took the hand and stood up, dusting the sand off his pants. "Let's see if we can get that poison out of your system." He smiled. "Then we'll find the Sage."

With a pat on the shoulder, Danny headed back down the beach toward Koto and Ninsar. Tyler watched for a moment, a fleeting sadness filling his heart. He hoped, for Danny's sake and his own, that they could make it to the Sage in time.

Eight

It was nearly mid-day after a long, restless night and Danny was on the verge of collapse. He'd spent the entire morning trying to remove the Zaba from the bag of boundlessness and when that didn't work, attempted to force the poison from Tyler's body. Both had been unsuccessful much to the frustration of all involved. Backing into the shade, Danny flopped down on his back in the dry leaves, staring up at the green canopy.

"I don't think I can do it," he said, the annoyance clear in his voice. "I need a break."

Tyler took a seat beside him. He was disappointed it hadn't worked, but somehow not surprised. With Danny's health deteriorating and the complicated nature of the spells, he knew it was a long shot to begin with. It wasn't like either of them had received any magical training or even had the slightest clue what they were doing. Koto could only offer so much help before the rest had to be done through trial and error. The problem was that neither of them knew what was going wrong with the spells, just that they weren't working.

Looking down at his chest, Tyler ran his fingers over the black veins of toxin spreading over his skin. Overnight they had grown, stretching further across his body. The marks were painful to the touch. He could feel a low fever persisting through his body that had nothing to do with the intense heat of the sun. A deep sluggishness seemed to permeate his every move, seeping into his very bones. The Zaba hadn't been kidding when she said it wouldn't take long for the toxin to take effect.

"I'm sorry, Tyler," Danny said, turning toward him.

"Don't be," Tyler sighed in reply, forcing himself to smile. "It was a lot to ask."

"We'll probably need more than one mage to pull it off," Koto added, sitting down with them. "Zaba poison is inherently magical and the bag has an extremely powerful enchantment on it. I wouldn't be surprised if even the most skilled in the academy couldn't do it alone.

Healing magic is a rare art and not a gift all can call upon." He glanced over to Danny. "It was a big job to ask of you. Don't feel bad."

"Yeah," Danny replied with a small scoff. "I'm still gonna feel shitty about it."

For a long while they sat there in the shade trying to rest and cool off from the heat of the midday sun. Tyler could feel the anxiety creeping into his chest knowing that he didn't have very long to live. Without outside help he'd be gone by the end of the week. Judging by their surroundings, they'd be lucky to make it to the mainland within that time frame. After that, who knew what waited for them. The chain of islands could lead them to a port city or to the middle of nowhere, an endless forest full of more monsters and problems. Neither Koto nor Ninsar seemed to have any idea where they were and Tyler hadn't thought to steal a map from the castle before they were almost killed by Clay and his guard.

"Can you somehow call out to the Sage using your stone?" Tyler asked, remembering the thought again. "Maybe he can send help."

Danny opened his mouth to respond, but Koto cut him off. "Have you ever met the Sage?"

Danny tilted his head to the side in confusion. "No. Why?"

"Then you won't be able to contact him." Koto sighed, gazing out over the beach. "Those kinds of spells are only possible when you know the person well. At the very least you have to have spoken with him once. Without that, the magic will never find its target."

"I can try anyway," Danny declared, holding out the red stone once more. "He's seen me, I just didn't see him."

"Yes, you can try," Koto nodded with a sigh.

Danny pushed himself up and sat cross legged in the sand, holding the stone to his chest and closing his eyes. Tyler could hear him whispering under his breath, but was unable to make out the words. He was beginning to wonder if Danny knew more magic than he'd let on. Maybe the bandits back at the keep had stolen a few books on the subject. For a brief moment the stone began to glow, Tyler's heart beating faster. But just as fast it died away. Danny's brows furrowed together in frustration as he tried again, but this time the stone didn't react at all.

"Well," Koto sighed, "there was no harm in trying I guess."

"It's alright D– Tiragan," Tyler said, catching himself. "We'll figure it out."

Danny slumped back on the grass and sand with a huff. "I sure hope so. I really don't want you to die and steal all the drama I've been building up." His head turned to the side, looking down the beach.

Trying to find anything else to think about besides his impending doom, Tyler glanced over the beach, then back at Danny. His friend's attention was fixed on the long strip of white sand in front of them. Following his line of sight he saw Ninsar down by the water. She had stripped down to her undergarments and was wringing out the dress she'd been wearing. After their flight through the castle and her murdering a guard in the dungeon, it had become rather stained. Her blonde hair reflected the bright sunlight that kissed her pale skin. With her dress in her hands Tyler could make out the years of scars across her body, covering her back and shoulders. Most were small, but the worst around her wrists and neck had a sheen that made them visible even from afar. Danny's eyes were fixed on her, not in lust, but adoration. It was a look Tyler recognized.

There was a twinge of jealousy in his heart, but Tyler pushed it aside, not wanting to deal with that too. He'd been best friends with Danny for years, although this was the first time he'd shown an interest in anyone. It was natural of him to feel protective, especially when Ninsar treated him like he was an idiot all the time.

"Like the view?" he asked casually, gesturing toward Ninsar.

Danny blushed immediately. "It's not like that."

Tyler lifted an eyebrow, happy to pull attention away from his own cares. "I literally caught you two naked in your bedroom with your clothes on the ground."

"I still had my pants on!"

"That was it and just barely."

Danny sighed, pulling his eyes away from Ninsar. "It's stupid anyway."

"And?" Tyler asked. "That doesn't mean you can't talk about it." Danny remained quiet. "Look, I'm not going to judge you. I'm just curious. But if you don't want to talk about it, we don't have to. You seemed pretty confident back at the castle, so I didn't think it would be a big deal."

"Back at the castle it was something different."

"Different?"

"Well..." Danny glanced at Koto who was pretending not to listen although one of his ears had swiveled in their direction. "Clay sent the courtesans up to my room and I just thought it was their job, ya know?" He sighed. "It wasn't until afterward that I found out they were slaves."

"How could you have known?"

"Did you know?"

"I... well... I asked," Tyler admitted. "They were acting weird when I turned them down. But one of them was brave enough to speak up."

"Ninsar?"

"No." Tyler could feel the overwhelming guilt filling his stomach. "It was a guy named... Faus."

"Is he..."

"Yeah. He's the one that got killed by Clay for helping me."

There was a long silence as they both turned back toward the beach, neither of them wanting to delve any further into the subject. Faus' murder was only a handful of days behind them, but to Tyler it felt like it had just happened moments before. He thought about the man often, running hundreds of scenarios through his head about what he could have done differently to spare his life. Unfortunately no matter what he figured out, it always ended the same way. Faus was dead and there was nothing he could do to make it less his fault, not now anyway.

"I like her," Danny said, breaking the silence at last. He gestured an arm out toward Ninsar. "She's tough, sweet when she wants to be, and a fierce fighter." He glanced back up at Tyler. "Did you know it took nearly a dozen soldiers to finally capture her when she escaped her first owner?"

Tyler shook his head. "No."

"She was on the run for a couple of years before they finally caught her again somewhere in the north. Apparently Clay chose the courtesans for the castle himself." Danny's head lowered. "He chose her because she spit in his face."

"Yeah," Tyler sighed. "That sounds like something he'd be into."

"She's been playing her part well for the past year, doing everything she could to get just enough trust to escape once more. But Clay kept a close eye on her and it wasn't until we came along that she finally got a chance to get out of there for good."

"So you like her... are you going to ask her out then?"

Danny shook his head. "No. That's the stupid part."

"Why is it stupid?"

"What am I supposed to say?" He lowered his voice. "Hey, thanks for doing your job for me once because you were a slave, wanna date?"

"Okay, so it's a bit weird. But still." Tyler shrugged. "You don't know until you try I guess."

"I can't. Look at me." He gestured to himself. "I'm a ticking time-bomb. I've got maybe three to four weeks left in me max. Why would she even entertain the idea of being romantic with me? At best she'll just get a week out of me and then have to take care of me until I die, like some invalid." He picked up a rock and chucked it out into the sand. "It's too late for that kind of stuff now."

Tyler reached out and put a hand on his shoulder, forcing Danny to look at him. "It's not too late. In fact, now's the perfect time."

"How do you figure that?"

"This is going to sound crude, but... if not now, when? What have you got to lose?"

Danny stared at him for a long moment.

"Even if everything goes terribly wrong, at least you took the chance while you had it, right?" Tyler swallowed his jealousy for a moment and pointed out toward Ninsar. "Just go tell her how you feel. You can't sit around waiting for your life to land in your lap, you've got to take the chance and go get it yourself. If you don't tell people what you want, how are they ever going to know?"

"You're right," Danny said with a nod. "I'm just scared of what she'll say."

"Then be scared," Tyler replied. "But do it anyway."

They held each other's gaze for a moment before Danny nodded. "Alright. I'll go make a fool of myself I guess." He paused. "And... it doesn't bother you?"

"Not at all," Tyler lied. "I hope it goes well."

Danny pushed himself to his feet and stretched. Ninsar looked up from the waves and smiled at him. Waving back to her he gave one last glance in Tyler's direction.

"You know," he sighed, looking a bit nervous, "that thing you said about telling people what you want?"

"Yeah?"

"Maybe... Maybe you should take your own advice... when you get back home that is." He paused, taking a deep breath to steady himself. "Tell your mom you don't want to go to school. And... tell her some other things too."

Tyler felt an odd combination of nervousness and irritation all at once. "I don't know what you mean," he replied curtly, lying through his teeth.

"I think you do, Tyler." He shrugged, a smile on his face. "It doesn't take a mind reader to see how you feel or what you're hiding." Leaning down close with his back to Koto he whispered, "And open your eyes. There's more happening in this world than you think, if only you'd just look and maybe let go of the old one a little bit."

With that, he patted Tyler on the shoulder and headed down the beach to Ninsar.

Nine

By the end of the day the four of them had managed to cross two of the islands, the sun sinking below the horizon as they paddled the last stretch of water onto the third. Being in the siren infested waters made Tyler nervous, but not getting off the island meant he would die, so he chose the sirens. They swam as fast as they could, taking breaks on the small rocks that jutted above the turquoise sea as they went. Despite their initial exhaustion, they were making better progress than anticipated. It turned out that all the islands seemed to be full of fruit, so finding food wasn't a problem and the sugar kept them energized. The high towers of dark stone that jutted above the canopies also meant that fresh water wasn't hard to locate either, the cold stones acting as a sort of condensation capture that resulted in small pools and waterfalls. If their problems weren't so dire, Tyler would have easily agreed to an extended stay on the islands just to relax and recuperate for as long as they wanted. It was a veritable paradise with its only downside being the murderous mermaids. But, as lazing about wasn't an option, he forced himself and everyone else forward at a breakneck pace.

Still dripping with saltwater, Tyler trudged up the beach to the treeline, scoping out a place to stay for the night. Behind him Danny and Ninsar were helping each other out of the surf, the waves crashing against their legs. It seemed his talk with her had gone well and they'd been nigh inseparable for the rest of the day. There was still a slight jealousy on Tyler's side, but he was happy for Danny. They'd spent so many years together as best friends that he figured it was only natural. A voice in the back of his mind told him it might be something more, but he shoved it down like he always did. He had enough problems on his plate already and dealing with that seemed ridiculous given the circumstances. After all, if they didn't find magical help in the next couple of days, he was going to be dead anyway. So what did it matter? Maybe if he survived he'd have a breakdown about it later, but that was a problem for another day. Then, after all that, he'd have to find a way to explain it to his mom, if he ever managed to break the spell she was under and get back home that was.

Tyler startled as he felt a hand on his shoulder, pulling him from his thoughts. He turned around to see Koto standing behind him, the same concerned look on his face as usual.

"You alright?"

"Yeah," Tyler replied too quickly. "Why wouldn't I be?"

Koto pointed to the trees. "You've been standing here staring intensely into the woods for almost a minute. I thought something was wrong or that you saw something strange."

Embarrassment flushed into his cheeks. "Sorry," Tyler replied, wrapping his hand over the opposite elbow. "Just lost in thought I guess."

He looked up at Koto, seeing the concern in his sea green eyes. They were kind of pretty now that he thought about it. There was something nice about Koto always seeming to be concerned about his well-being. Lots of people asked him how he was doing on a daily basis back home, but they were never really looking for a true answer, just a polite response. Danny and Clay were the only people who ever really cared how he felt, but they'd known each other for years. Recently both of them seemed too wrapped up in their own problems to worry about him. He'd only known Koto for a couple of weeks and already the man gave him the impression that he genuinely cared. It was a strange realization that made him feel anxious, suspicious, and light all at the same time.

"You're doing it again."

"Sorry!" Tyler shook his head, turning away from Koto. "I'm looking for food," He lied. "We need a place to stay for the night and something to eat."

"People from your world are very odd," Koto replied, lifting an eyebrow and giving him a once over. "But interesting. It's been quite the experience traveling with you."

"Thanks?" Tyler wasn't sure if it was a compliment or passive aggression. "Everything here is insane... so, same I guess."

"I know you aren't overly fond of this world." Koto's voice softened a bit as he gazed out over the sea, the moonlight reflecting on the water. "But I hope it's at least been enjoyable in some small way." He shook his head immediately. "What am I saying? You're standing in front of me with Zaba toxin seeping into your body. I apologize."

"No, it's okay. I think if I was here under different circumstances, I'd be having a lot more fun." He reached a hand up and ran it over the rubbery flesh on his chest where the toxin had touched him. The sensation was deeply unsettling. "Sometimes I wish I could just stay here and fall in love with this place like Danny has. This world is incredible and everything I've ever fantasized about, but if I make the decision to stay here, to be that selfish when others are counting on me... am I any better than Clay?"

Koto placed a hand on his shoulder. "Clay is hurting people. Who would you hurt by staying here and living a life you want to live?"

"My mom," Tyler sighed, running a hand through his wet hair. "She's got my whole future planned out. College, successful job, wife, children, the whole nine yards. But I don't want any of that." He hung his head, kicking at the sand. "My father walked out on us when I was a kid and we've struggled ever since. I know she just wants me to have a better life than what she got and I feel like an ass telling her that her plans aren't what I want. Not that I don't want a nice life, but just not the one she has planned for me, ya know? I want to build it myself and make it my own."

"I think I understand," Koto replied with a nod. "All parents want what *they* think is best for their children. But sometimes what they have planned isn't going to work for the people we become."

"Yeah... but how do I tell her? I'm afraid I'll sound like I don't appreciate all the hard work she's done trying to raise me. All the long nights working overtime and being on call at the hospital nearly every day of the week. She's sacrificed her whole life to take care of me."

"That was her choice," Koto said calmly. "Now you have to make your own and build the life you want to live. If she respects you, she'll understand."

Tyler looked up at Koto. "Do you really think so?"

"You're a capable person, although a bit inexperienced, but that's normal for one your age. All you can do is what you think is best. Fulfilling your mother's dreams is not your job as a child. You have to be true to yourself and she can share that happiness if she wants to." His voice darkened as he turned his gaze away from Tyler. "Parents shouldn't use their kids to make up for their own shortcomings. Children aren't tools or pets, they are people."

The look in Koto's eyes was enough to break Tyler's heart. He knew Koto was thinking of his father as he spoke, the hurt in his voice all too clear. There was more there too, the crushing grief of having taken his own father's life and never getting the chance to set things right. For the first time since he'd set foot in Bramoria, he counted himself lucky. His mother was still alive and she loved him, at least he hoped she did once her memories were returned. Although it might not make her happy for him to finally tell the truth, at least he had the choice to say it. If he could somehow rescue her from Clay, he might even get the opportunity to say what he'd been thinking for some time and get it off his chest at last.

"You're right," Tyler replied at last. "I need to start being more honest with people and... and myself."

Koto smiled. "Start with yourself and work your way up from there. There's no rush."

"I mean, there's a little bit of a rush." Tyler glanced down at the black veins across his chest. "Maybe I can start with something that I've known for a while, but have been afraid to say out loud."

"What's that?"

"I think I mi–"

"Tyler! Koto!" Ninsar's shrill voice cried from down the moonlit beach. "Help me! Something's wrong with Tiragan!"

Whipping around Tyler saw Ninsar leaning over Danny's body that was convulsing in the sand. His heart nearly stopped beating as he saw the jerky movements of his friend's body. He'd seen it before and it wasn't a good sign.

Feeling a hand on his arm, Tyler broke from his stupor, dragged by Koto down the beach toward Danny. Skidding to a halt in the sand, Tyler dropped down next to him on his knees, trying to hold him down as he shook. His jaw was clenched shut and foam was leaking from the corners of his mouth.

"He's having a seizure," he said, the panic rising in his chest. He tried to remember what Danny's mother had told him all those years ago. "Help me get his mouth open and hand me a piece of leather! Anything to keep his teeth apart!"

Koto pulled his belt off, slipping off everything attached to it. Both he and Tyler leaned down and pried Danny's mouth open. As soon as the leather was in they let go, his teeth clamping down on it. Tyler reached down and pushed Danny onto his side, trying to make sure he didn't choke on his own saliva.

"What do we do?" Ninsar sobbed, her hands shaking as she stared.

"I... I don't know," Tyler replied, all the knowledge slipping from his head in an instant. "He's only done this once before when he was really sick. He must be worse off than we thought." The panic caused his heart to pound, the Zaba toxin pulsing through his system even faster. All his thoughts were fuzzy and the vertigo was getting worse with each passing heartbeat. "We need help! I can't do anything for him, none of us can!"

Koto and Ninsar stared at him with blank panicked faces. Tyler looked down at Danny, watching his body continue to shake and quiver in the sand. A flash or red caught his eye as the mage stone slipped from

Danny's pocket and landed next to his knee. In an instant Tyler knew what he had to do. He reached down and grabbed the stone, lifting it high and closing his eyes.

"No!" Koto yelled. "You can't do tha–"

But it was too late.

The stone trembled in his hand and grew to a brilliant red, the light shining through his eyelids. With a streak of fiery pain erupting through his body, Tyler felt his consciousness ripped from reality and he was thrown into the starscape void once again. However, this time the stars were vibrating strangely and everything had taken on a reddish glow. There was a deep unsettling vibration echoing through his body, not the usual unending silence. For a moment he thought the magic hadn't worked, then a figure appeared in front of him once more, the blue light of his staff nearly crushed by the red hue that swallowed everything.

"Danny and I are both dying! We won't make it to you in time if you don't help us!"

The figure's lips moved, but Tyler heard no sound.

"Please! I can't let him die! Not after everything he's been through! Even you said that's not how this story goes."

Again, moving lips but no sound. The pain wracking Tyler's body was growing unbearable as he doubled over, clutching his belly. It felt like the magic would tear him apart. He fell forward onto the hard invisible surface, his hand reaching for the Sage. There was no one else in all of Bramoria that could save them now.

As his vision began to fade, he looked up one last time. Fiery blue wings erupted from the Sage's back, forcing away all the red in the starscape. Tyler felt a coolness wash over his skin, but it wasn't enough to stop the unyielding pain in his body.

"Please..."

That was his last word before his hand dropped to the ground and his world went dark.

Ten

It was dragons again. Why was it always dragons? At least this time they were fighting each other instead of trying to kill him.

Tyler once again found himself in a field of green grass, trees, and open plain covering the vast hills around him. High above a pair of dragons flew, both of them roaring and clawing as they crashed into one another. Spouts of flame erupted in the sky, the flashes drawing the attention of the others on the ground. This time it wasn't soldiers, but ordinary looking people and a few faces he recognized. Danny, Ninsar, and Koto were all there looking up into the sky. Beyond them he could just make out a few of the mages he'd seen at the academy, their long flowing robes giving them away as they stood idly by.

Tyler turned his head back to the sky, watching the dragons try to tear each other apart. One was a brightly colored green dragon, but instead of fire shooting from its mouth, it seemed to bellow a misty blue haze as it reacted to a vicious bite on its wing. The other was dark and surrounded by roiling smoke, the same that he'd seen attacking the villages. It clawed and snapped its jaws, looking for anything to find purchase on and bring the green dragon down. With its front claws it grabbed the green dragon's wings, locking itself around the other's body. Unable to keep themselves aloft, the pair began to plummet toward the ground, gaining speed at an incredible rate.

The bodies collided with the hillside, grass and dirt flying in all directions. Tyler felt the impact rumble through the soles of his feet followed by a deep boom. Roars of rage and pain filled the air around him, but the people nearby just watched, their lips unmoving. The dragons continued their fight, each plume of fire taking out more innocent bystanders that stood by. The mist from the green dragon seemed to dissolve flesh the moment it touched one of the onlookers, their bodies melting as it wafted over them. As they worked their way across the field the scene slowly evolved into a massacre.

"Phenomenal creatures, aren't they?" a familiar baritone voice said from behind him.

Tyler spun on his heel to see Clay standing there in his black armor, the onyx colored stone gleaming on his chest. He wore a smirk composed of pure malice as he looked on at the fight taking place. Lifting a hand he pointed at the dragons, the mage stone on his chest flashing. Suddenly the darker dragon began to swell, the roiling smoke around its form doubling in size. The claws extended, the fangs grew, and the muscles bulged against the scales. In a matter of moments it was nearly twice the size of the green dragon. Even so, the green didn't back down. Instead it reeled its head back and let out another blast of acidic haze at the massive creature.

"Such prideful creatures," Clay chuckled. "No wonder they aren't around anymore. Pride without power is a recipe for failure."

"Why are you doing this?" Tyler asked. Nobody around him had reacted to Clay's presence. "Call it off before they kill everyone!"

Clay just smiled. "Why would I do that? We're having so much fun."

"What's wrong with you? What happened to the Clay I knew?" Tyler knew the words would have no effect on him, but he had to try.

"That's an easy one. He's dead." Clay glanced back toward the battle. "I killed him with my own hands. He was weak and afraid to stand up for himself. Not that he didn't try once or twice, but that didn't last long." His gaze narrowed on Tyler. "Especially since his so-called friends refused to help him in his most desperate hour. He was easy to squash."

"So what? You're just going to kill everyone in Bramoria to prove that I'm a terrible person, is that it?"

"For someone who's spent their whole life focusing on school, you sure are stupid." He waved his black metallic hand through the air, a small sphere of darkness forming above it. "It wouldn't do me much good to have an empty kingdom to rule, would it?" With a flick of his wrist he sent the sphere higher into the air, energy coalescing around it as it grew. "Once I draw the Sage out and kill him, Bramoria will be mine to rule forever." He glanced back at Tyler. "Then I'll send you home to deal with your shattered reality alone, something I've had to live with for years."

"You're the one controlling the dragons..." Tyler muttered, the realization finally setting in. "That's why those parts of the books were missing!"

"Again, your stupidity knows no bounds. Any fool could have figured that out in five minutes and yet it took you nearly a week."

"I won't let you get away with this," Tyler growled, stepping up into Clay's face. "Do you hear me!"

Clay laughed. "You have no stone, you are dying, and you are lost. You are no threat to me." He lunged forward and grabbed Tyler by the neck, lifting him off the ground with his gauntlet clad hand. "And even if you somehow miraculously survive, you're no match for me." His eyes narrowed. "Especially once I have Danny on my side."

"He won't fall for your tricks!" Tyler gasped, struggling to free himself. "He'll never join you now that he knows what you've become!"

"Oh, I think he will." Clay brought Tyler's face close to his, a maniacal smile pulling at his lips. "And now, it's time to end this little nightmare of yours."

Clay threw Tyler to the ground, his body crashing against stone and earth as he rolled through the grass. Trying to force the air back into his lungs, he glanced back at Clay. Both of his hands were raised high in the air, the massive black sphere swirling above them. Chilling laughter filled the hills as he hurled the magic in Tyler's direction. The sphere whizzed through the air, not even giving him enough time to close his eyes as he threw an arm up to shield himself.

A flash of turquoise blue erupted in front of Tyler, the sphere colliding with it. The blast nearly deafened him and a burst of hot wind filled with debris surrounded him. Pulling his arm down he saw a large bird floating in front of him with wings outspread and a massive fanned tail of many colors like a peacock. The sphere was gone, the magic blocked by the creature that now stood between him and Clay. A soft song filled the air all around him that could only be described as ethereal. Tyler glanced out to the field noticing that even the dragons had stopped fighting and had turned their attention in his direction.

"So," Clay hissed. "Now he sends his pet to protect the fool." He lifted his hands once more, another sphere of darkness forming. "Then I'll kill it too!"

Before the sphere could be released once more, a shrill cry filled the air and turquoise flames erupted all around Tyler, obscuring his vision. He felt a gentle warmth as he was cut off from the world of his dreams and his vision faded into darkness.

"Tyler," a voice said softly, hollow and far away. "Please wake up."

A deep seated soreness was all Tyler could feel throughout his entire body. All of his limbs felt too heavy to move and his eyelids didn't want to listen to his commands. The warmth from his dream still filled his chest. It was comforting and peaceful, making him never want to leave the bliss in between sleep and wakefulness. There time stood still and everything was okay. There he was safe.

"Please, Tyler," the voice said again, this time a bit closer.

He didn't want to wake, but he felt himself pulled toward consciousness nonetheless. Struggling against it, he tried to stay where he was. He just needed more time to himself, only a sliver of forever to be at peace for once.

"He moved!" The voice became more familiar, the excitement clear in its intonation.

Against his will, Tyler felt his eyes flutter, the harshness of the world creeping back into his senses.

"Tyler? Can you hear me?"

A face appeared over him with dark hair and tall familiar ears. It was Koto.

"There you are," Koto said, breathing a sigh of relief as he sat back on his heels. "You had me worried there for a bit, ya know?"

Tyler grimaced as the bright green light from above seemed to pierce straight into his brain. Squinting he glanced up, just able to make out the dense canopy of leaves high above him. But they were different than he remembered. Instead of palms and jungle flora, he saw those more similar to what he was used to back home. His nose caught the scent of cool rich earth and rotting leaves. Turning his head to the side he noticed he was lying on a bed of moss and leaves, a few bright green ferns poking up nearby. Wherever he was, it wasn't on the island chain he'd passed out on.

"What... What's going on?" he struggled to say, turning his attention back to Koto. "Where are we?"

"Safe thanks to you," Koto smiled. His brows furrowed together as he leaned back over Tyler. "What you did was stupid and reckless. No one can use another's mage stone. That's a good way to get yourself killed." He sighed, sitting back once more. "But somehow you did it and you got us the help we needed."

"Then... the Sage came?"

"He did. And he took Tiragan with him."

"What?!" Tyler sat up, the sudden movement making his entire world spin.

Koto caught him before he crashed back to the ground. "Woah! Take it easy! You've been out for a couple of days. You need to slow down."

"Why did you let him take Danny?" Tyler was furious. "We don't even know if he's the good guy yet!"

"You wouldn't still be here if he wasn't." Koto reached up and pulled Tyler's shirt aside. "See for yourself."

Tyler looked down. The wound on his side was gone, a fresh pink scar taking the place of the purple festering flesh that had been there before. The spider web of toxin was still there, but pink as well instead of its usual black. He reached down and ran a finger over it, feeling the smooth texture of the scars now lacing over his chest. Somehow the toxin was gone.

"What... What happened? How did you get rid of it?""

"I didn't. The Sage did. Or well, his bird did."

"His bird?"

"Yeah," Koto nodded. "He came right to us on fiery wings, both the Sage and his giant phoenix. The Sage took one look at Tiragan and scooped him up, telling us to come to him at his castle amongst the Dravin Peaks. He then said something to his bird that in a language I didn't understand, but he teleported out before I could ask any questions." Koto helped Tyler into a more comfortable position, leaning him up against a tree. "Then the bird carried all three of us here in a single night before he turned to you. I wasn't sure what he was going to do, the toxin had gotten a lot worse since you tried to use Tiragan's stone. But when he leaned down to you he burst into blue flame, surrounding your entire body. In a flash he was gone and the toxin burned out of your system." He glanced back at the scars, reaching out but pulling his hand back at the last moment. "That was almost two days ago."

"So... it was real..." Tyler murmured to himself.

"What was?"

"The dream..." Tyler looked back up at Koto. "I had a dream that a fiery bird saved me from Clay. He was trying to kill me." The dream suddenly came rushing back to him along with the realizations he'd made during it. "Clay is the one controlling the dragons!" he cried, trying to get up once more.

Koto pushed him back down. "You need to rest. Give yourself a moment to recover!"

"We don't have time!" Tyler continued, his panic rising. "You don't understand! He's going to try to kill the Sage and take Danny away!"

"The Sage has been around for over a thousand years. Nobody can kill him. He's as much a part of Bramoria as the mountains and the rivers."

"Clay is *creating* dragons, Koto!" He stared the man in the eye. "Is that something the Sage can do?"

Koto was silent for a long moment. "No."

"He's in danger. Clay has the book, the academy, and the Divinarae under his control. There's no telling what kind of power he's uncovered." Tyler paused for a moment, trying to force himself to breathe. "We have to stop him before he destroys everything. He told me himself he won't stop until the entire world bows at his feet. And... and he said he wants to use Danny to do it."

"Tiragan is safe for the time being," Koto said, placing a firm hand on Tyler's shoulder. "If Clay could kill the Sage at any time, he would have done it already. At the very least we still have some time to reach him and warn him what's going on." He gave Tyler a serious look and a firm squeeze on the shoulder. "Until then I need you to take it easy and try not to panic. That's not going to help anyone. I believe you and Ninsar will too once you tell her."

"I already do," her voice replied.

Tyler looked up to see Ninsar coming around a tree into the small clearing they were in. She looked tired and run down, but there was a fierceness in her eyes, more so than before.

"The king is capable of a lot more than he lets on," she continued, directing her gaze at Koto. "Courtesans hear many things and most of them secret under pain of death. I don't know any specifics, but what you say doesn't surprise me and that is proof enough for me."

Koto sighed, hanging his head. "I suppose that means we need to get moving?" She nodded. Pushing himself to his feet he held out a hand to Tyler. "So much for your recovery."

Taking Koto's hand, Tyler was pulled back to standing for the first time in a couple of days and the vertigo nearly put him in the dirt again. Leaning against a tree to get his legs under control he looked to the other two.

"So where are we?"

Ninsar answered. "From what I can see, we're a day or two south of Zoethaven, which lies on the edge of the Blightwood." She glanced at

Koto. "It's a pretty big port city and the last before the untamed wilds of the north. We'd best stock up there with what we can. There won't be anything else until we reach the Sage."

"How do you know all this?" he asked. "I thought you were a palace slave?"

"I wasn't always a palace slave," she grinned, a hand placed on her hip. "In fact, the first time I ran away I started to make quite a name for myself before I got caught again. Of course, it didn't help that the only people who'd hire an ex slave were criminals. I got a bit more of a reputation than I could stay ahead of, even after I tried to lay low."

"I never would have suspected–"

"That's every man's problem," she replied, cutting him off. "Nobody expects the soft spoken subservient girls to be capable and deadly. They just see them as a stupid toy to play with."

Koto's ears flattened against his head. "I didn't mean that."

"Maybe *you* didn't, but society has taught you to make assumptions, just like every other person out there. But I'll give you both a word of advice." Her smile widened. "While we're out here in the wilds, you should assume everyone is capable, no matter what they look like." She glared at Tyler specifically. "Even the children here are taught to fend for themselves."

He may not have liked Ninsar much or what she was implying, but Tyler had to respect her. Their escape from the castle wouldn't have been possible without her and he had watched her kill a man with nothing but a dagger. She was not to be trifled with.

"Are we ready then?" she asked, turning back toward where she'd stepped out of the forest. "I'd like to sleep in a bed at least one more time before I die."

Gathering all the strength he could muster, Tyler took his first steps. "Yeah. Let's get out of here. We need to save Da–... I mean Tiragan."

"Just a second," Koto said, reaching down to the ground and picking up a round leather sack the size of a football. He held it out to Tyler. "This is for you to hold onto."

Tyler looked it over. "What is it?"

Koto pulled a section of the leather away revealing a dark purple stone that looked like it was made of smoky amethyst. "I think it's the phoenix," he replied, tapping a claw against the crystalline surface. There was a soft ring that echoed through it that reminded Tyler of the song he'd heard in his dreams. "It was all that was left once he healed you. I don't know much about phoenixes, but I think this is something you need to hold on to. At least until we get to the Sage." He gave Tyler a once over. "Usually I'd offer to take it for you and I can't explain it... but it feels wrong for me to carry it."

Nodding, Tyler took the bag from Koto and slung it over his shoulders. It weighed almost nothing. Immediately it began to warm against his back, the relaxing feeling spreading through his body and melting some of his pain and vertigo away.

"I'll take care of it," he replied. "It's the least I can do since it saved my life."

"Come on boys," Ninsar said, waving for them to follow. "We have a lot of ground to cover if we want to stop this world from falling apart."

Eleven

Due to Tyler's slow pace, it took them nearly two days to reach the town of Zoethaven. Thankfully the land was relatively flat and the woods open with little underbrush, making their travel easy. It was late afternoon on the second day when they finally broke through the edge of the forest on a small rise above the town. Laid out in front of them was a crescent shaped city pressed against a small bay with white stone walls surrounding it down to the water. All the buildings had been whitewashed, creating a kind of rich glow as the sun streamed over the town's streets. Docks reached out into the bay, an array of ships in all sizes moored in the cerulean water glimmering in the sun. A single tower, easily five stories high, rose up in the center of the town above the rest of the buildings. At the very top was a hovering crystal, much like the one at the bandit hideout where they'd found Danny, catching the light, casting a rainbow of color down to the streets below. It was a mesmerizing sight.

"Wow," Tyler breathed, looking over the pristine city below them. It looked like something out of a book, which felt stupid considering he was *actually* inside a book.

"It's beautiful from up here," Ninsar replied at his side. "But don't let it fool you. This is a port town and the northernmost trade hub in the kingdom. It's full of pirates, thieves, and slavers. Don't let your guard down or you'll end up somewhere you don't want to be." She turned and looked back at Koto. "Especially you. Veordya are rare in these parts and they fetch a high price on the slave market. There's lots of people out there who like *exotic* pets."

Koto's ears swiveled back, his off-hand automatically going to the hilt of his sword. His other was still wrapped up and cradled in a makeshift sling. It seemed like months since they'd fought the Fossars that wounded him, but in reality it had only been a couple of weeks. Tyler hoped once they got to the Sage they'd finally be able to heal him so he could use his bow again. They would be much safer when he could fight to his full potential again.

"I'll be sure to keep my eyes open," he replied, giving a grateful nod to Ninsar. He glanced down at the tower. "Is there a teleportation circle in this town?"

Ninsar sighed. "Yes. And the king is sure to have his spies on the lookout for us."

"He won't need them," Koto said, shaking his head. "The Divinarae will show him where we are. I wouldn't be surprised if someone was already down there waiting for us. We'll need to get out of sight as fast as possible."

All three of them looked back down at the port city of Zoethaven, the clean streets and shimmering crystal losing their luster with a single statement. If Clay's minions were waiting for them, Tyler had no idea how they were going to get through unseen. As he lifted his gaze to the northwest he saw the Blightwood Koto had told him about. The trees were dark and obscured by a thick mist that seemed to hang over them despite the blazing sun. Hills and valleys filled the forest, only a single winding river cutting any sort of path through the trees. Beyond it, hazy in the distance, were the snow capped mountains he assumed to be the Dravin Peaks. That's where the Sage was waiting for them. The more he stared, the more the distance looked impossible to traverse. One thing was certain, if they didn't stop for supplies, they wouldn't even make it through the woods, much less over the mountains. The city would be dangerous, but without it they had no hope without it. Tyler heaved a deep sigh.

"Alright," he said, trying to gather his courage. "Let's wait till dark to go in and we'll leave before it gets light. Hopefully nobody sees us."

Koto nodded in his direction, his tail flicking nervously behind him. "That's a good plan."

"Follow my lead," Ninsar replied, waving them forward. "I think I know a place we can stay that's out of the way."

A COUPLE HOURS LATER Tyler found himself standing outside of the most garish building he'd ever seen. The entire facade was covered in carved scrolling that had been gilded gold and shimmered in the lamplight. Every window, door, and shade was a different color, all painted as brightly as possible to attract the attention of sailors making their way into the city from the docks. The noise from inside was raucous and happy, filled with music as the stench of alcohol and sweat wafted out of the front door. From above he could hear a few noises coming from open windows that left little to the imagination. Tyler's eyes fell to a pair of swinging doors at the entrance with a giant clam painted on them, a golden pearl held in the center of its shells.

"The Gilded Clam?!" Tyler turned back to Ninsar. He couldn't believe what he was seeing. "This is a brothel, isn't it?"

"What gave it away?" she asked, gesturing to the front porch area where several couples were busy getting very well *acquainted*, some of them with no shame. "I worked here for a little while." She glanced over the place with a small smile as if recalling fond memories. "I was the bouncer."

Tyler shook his head. After seeing what she'd done to that guard back at the castle, it didn't surprise him. "But why here of all places? I thought we wanted to stay away from thieves and pirates. Don't they frequent these places?"

"Nobody is going to be looking for us here and we'll be out of sight," she replied. "The king will expect us to lie low in the most out of the way place we can find. This is right in the center of town, everybody comes here."

Koto snickered to himself, but Tyler wasn't having it.

"There are too many people going in and out of here for us to be noticed *and* they have some of the best food in town. It's the perfect place to stay. I also happen to know where all the secret hiding places are if somebody comes looking for us. This is the safest place we can be."

"You're sure?" Tyler asked, nervous about the idea of staying in a brothel.

"Believe me, I know this place well. If you need someone to disappear in this city, this is where you go."

Tyler raised an eyebrow. "I'm not sure I like how that sounds."

"Well, this is your choice." She gestured out to the rest of the city behind them. "Or you're free to go figure it out on your own, but I'm staying here for the night. And then, in the morning, I'm going after Tiragan." She glanced over Tyler's shoulder at Koto. "You gonna argue with me too?"

"No ma'am."

"I'm not argu–" Tyler began.

"Good," she said, cutting him off. "Then let's get inside before we're killed in the street by the king's hounds or a drunk sailor looking for a fight."

Turning away from him, Ninsar walked up the stairs to the front door, leaving them both standing in the road.

"Come on," Koto said. "We shouldn't separate."

"Why does she hate me so much?"

"She doesn't hate you," Koto replied with a smile. "She just doesn't like you very much."

As they stepped through the swinging doors behind Ninsar, Tyler was struck by a nearly solid wall of perfume, smoke, and liquor. He coughed and blinked a few times, trying to adjust to the sudden shift in atmosphere. The first thing that caught his attention was the sheer size of the place. From the front it looked like a normal tavern with other businesses on either side. But once inside he realized that it must have sprawled into the neighborhood behind it for some way. The massive room was filled with tables and chairs, a large glossy bar made of dark purple wood on the far end. Bottles and barrels covered the back wall while two bartenders were busy rushing out orders to their scantily clad staff. No less than four dozen customers filled the space and for every two of them there was at least one courtesan. Both men and women of many races paraded through the space looking to please any customer with the coin to hire their services. There were a couple Veordya like Koto, at least one male of the lizard people that he didn't know the name of, and several others that he'd never even seen before.

Pulling his eyes away from the courtesans, he glanced up, noticing three large golden chandeliers with brightly burning flames along their edges. The room was open to the second floor, a walkway encircling the room with a number of doors along the path. Several people were either being escorted up to a room, leaving, or rushing about to change bedsheets and freshen the rooms for the next customer. There was even a pair of large swinging doors at the back of the tavern where food was coming out. Tyler laid his eyes on a heaping platter of roasted meats and cheeses on one of the nearby tables, his mouth watering instantly. For a moment he'd been distracted by the courtesans, but the food was what he really wanted after spending days either unconscious or hiking through the woods.

"Stick close to me," Ninsar commanded. "I'll get us rooms for the night and some food. We should probably stay out of sight as much as possible."

"Good idea," Koto replied, his ears turned down to block out some of the noise. "I wouldn't mind something a bit more peaceful."

Ninsar pointed to a free table in the far corner. "Go sit over there while I get things going. If we're lucky, we won't run into the owner. She's not here usually, so we should be fi–"

"NINSAR DELONDRA!" a gruff voice bellowed over the noise.

The entire crowd went quiet as a large woman with dark skin and flowing black braids stepped out from the kitchen, one of the bartenders on her heels looking worried. She wore dark pants and what Tyler could only describe as a white pirate's shirt, with an ornate golden belt around her waist. She wore no visible weapons, but around her neck set into a delicate gold chain was a glowing magenta stone that flared as her voice rang out over the crowd. Tyler immediately recognized it as a mage stone.

"Oh... uh hey Zimu!" Ninsar said nervously. She looked wildly uncomfortable. "How... How's business?"

"Business?" Zimu cried back. "Business?! That's what you say to me after you destroy half of my bar and get carried away in chains?" She stomped across the room until she was less than a foot from Ninsar, her thick arms crossed over her chest. "You disappear for two years and you just waltz back in here like nothing happened?"

The entire room was staring at the pair of them. Ninsar looked on the edge of vomiting as she stared up at the woman in front of her. Tyler was trying to think of anything to say to stop a fight from breaking out. But just as he opened his mouth, Zimu smiled and pulled Ninsar into a big hug.

"Don't go doing anything like that again!" Zimu said, crushing Ninsar against her ample bosom. The tension in the room eased almost instantly. After a long moment the noise began to build once more as she pulled Ninsar away from her. "I've been worried sick about you, child! When you didn't come back I assumed the worst. What happened? Who were those people that took you away?"

Ninsar smiled, a breath of relief escaping her lips. "Bounty hunters," she replied. "They'd been looking for me since I escaped my previous owner. However, it seems he wasn't the highest bidder this time. They took me back and sold me to the king himself as a courtesan. Needless to say it has not been the most pleasant."

"How a nice girl like you got caught up in the slave trade, I'll never understand."

"Being young and foolish at the time didn't help."

Zimu nodded with a smile, clapping a hand on Ninsar's tiny shoulder. "But here you are, free again! Come over here and sit with me, we need to catch up."

"I can't," Ninsar said, pulling herself from Zimu's grasp. "At least not right now." She leaned in close. "We have reason to believe we might be pursued by the king's men and we're on our way to see the Sage."

Even though the word wasn't uttered loudly, a handful of heads still turned their direction at the sound of it. Zimu's eyes flashed magenta as she glared at them, the stone around her neck following suit. All of them turned back to their own business in an instant. Two of them seemed either annoyed or frightened by her and got up from their tables, leaving the brothel completely.

"Don't say that name here, it's not safe. There's a lot of mixed feelings about that guy right now thanks to the dragon attacks." She glanced at Tyler and Koto who were looking uncomfortable from the sudden attention. "But we'll talk about that later. You need someplace to stay I assume?"

"If you can. We can pay."

"Nonsense, child! You're family here." She pointed back toward the kitchen. "Go through the kitchen into the dormitory and take one of the guest rooms. I'll send someone back to take care of you all. I'll meet you there in a couple of hours. Business is booming and I'm afraid I have more on my plate than I can handle at the moment."

"Not to be a bother, but we need some supplies too," Ninsar said nervously. "I know it's a lot to ask, but we have gold."

"Please," Zimu laughed, waving her away. "Nobody here would turn down gold to run an errand, especially if it means not having to bolster another drunk sailor's ego." She glanced over to Koto and Tyler. "Men can be very sensitive about their masts, if you know what I mean."

Despite himself, Tyler smiled. He was trying to stay serious about their current predicament, but Zimu's character and tone of voice made him feel at home despite the unfamiliar environment, like the fun aunt that everyone always seemed to be talking about. Out of the corner of his eye he noticed a few of the patrons still staring at them. They needed to get out of sight before they were caught.

"Not to rush you," he said mostly to Zimu. "But we really shouldn't be seen any more than necessary."

"Of course," Zimu replied, shaking her head. "You know where to take them Ninsar, go ahead. I'll be back there soon. And I'll make sure you're not remembered," she said, giving a small wink.

"Thank's Zimu."

Ninsar motioned to Tyler and Koto, leading them to the back of the room. Zimu watched them go with a smile on her face. She reached up and clapped her hands twice, the stone around her neck glowing brightly once more.

"The drinks for the next hour are buy one, get one free!" she called, her voice magically amplified over the entire tavern. "Drink, be merry, and don't forget to tip your companions for a job well done!"

Raucous cheers filled the room as the three of them pushed through the crowd surging toward the bar and a pair of terrified looking bartenders. Without being noticed, they slipped through the large swinging doors of the kitchen and into the back of the brothel out of sight.

Twelve

The food was better than Tyler expected, brought to them by a short petite woman with an auburn beard and strong arms. She looked like she could easily break him in half, so Tyler didn't ask about the beard and made sure she was tipped well for the service. He made a mental note to ask Koto about the other races of people in Bramoria later. The money was easy to give away, after all, they'd stolen it from the castle's dungeon armory anyway, so he figured it would go to better use in the world with real people.

After they had eaten, three more courtesans were sent in by Zimu to go into town for the supplies they needed. Ninsar wrote out a list, dividing it into types of goods and splitting them among their hired help. Sending them off with the majority of their money, she came back and took a seat near the fireplace, propping her feet up on the mantle. Tyler had never seen her so relaxed, but even so there was a subtle nervousness about her. She constantly checked the door and the windows, her gaze never staying in one place for long. He wondered if she was worried about them being attacked, but he didn't want to ask. It was no secret that she didn't like him very much and he didn't want to seem like he was prying into her personal life, especially if it would just cause another one of her outbursts.

Koto, on the other hand, seemed perfectly at ease. After the good meal he flopped down on the bed closest to the fire and laced his fingers behind his head, staring up at the ceiling. For some reason, Tyler had the urge to go and sit with him, but he didn't know what they would talk about. It wasn't like he could ask about the weather or Koto's family, and being in a brothel was completely alien to Tyler, so that wouldn't be a topic of conversation. Still, since their time on the island he'd found himself wanting to spend more time with Koto. He couldn't quite put his finger on why he felt the urge, but it was there just the same. Maybe they were finally starting to feel like friends. That had to be it.

Before he could put much more thought into it, he heard the heavy footsteps of someone approaching their room. A loud knock at the door caused Ninsar to nearly jump out of her chair.

"It's me," Zimu's rich voice called from the other side of the door. "May I come in?"

Ninsar visibly relaxed, her hand coming off the hilt of her sword. "Of course!" She walked over and unlocked the door, pulling it open. "You do own the place you know."

"Politeness will get you a long way, child," Zimu smiled. She gave Ninsar a playful nudge in the shoulder. "Something you could probably stand to learn a bit more of."

Tyler had to stifle a snort. Ninsar shot a glare his way, but Zimu found it amusing.

"See," she said. "It sounds like they already know the truth as well."

Ninsar sighed, pushing the door closed. "Can we stop picking on me and get down to business? We don't have time for this."

"You should learn to relax a bit," she said, patting Ninsar on the shoulder before she walked over to a chair in the corner and took a seat. She took a long moment to get settled, taking out a pipe from her pocket and beginning to pack it with tobacco. "So, it seems you're all out here looking for the Sage." She glanced over them all. "Can I ask why you would be doing something so dangerous?"

"He has my friend," Tyler replied immediately. "And we need his help to stop Clay."

"Clay?"

"The king," Ninsar answered. "But Tiragan is my top priority."

"Really?" Zimu looked surprised, completely ignoring the comment about the king. "You're out here because of a man? I thought you had sworn off men after the last one got you into all that trouble with the slavers?"

"Yeah, I did."

"What changed?"

Ninsar looked up at Zimu with an exasperated sigh. "This one's too stupid to be bad."

A boisterous laugh filled the room as Zimu leaned forward in her chair, slapping a hand on her knee. "Child, you really stepped in it this time," she smiled. "The stupid and nice ones are the most dangerous. They'll get you every time, like a puppy looking for love." Leaning back in her chair she crossed her arms over her chest. "The amount of times I've lost good courtesans to dumb boys has cost me a fortune. And that's not even counting the freebies they got along the way."

"He's not stupid," Tyler cut in, annoyed that they would say such things about his best friend. "He's just not from Bramoria... and he's a bit... delusional sometimes."

Zimu nodded, but looked back at Ninsar. "So you're doing charity work now?"

"Anyway," Ninsar replied, glaring at the both of them. "He's sick and the Sage is taking care of him for the moment. We need to get to him before anything goes wrong. That and as I mentioned, we're on the run from the king."

"That explains the bounty hunters," Zimu nodded, striking a match and lighting her pipe.

Koto's ears perked up. "What bounty hunters?"

She took a deep pull before blowing out a bluish smoke that swirled through the air. "A trio of Lacerta came in asking some questions about an hour after you arrived. They didn't seem like the nicest type." Zimu's eyes narrowed, the stone around her neck flaring. "They tried getting rough with a couple of my people and I nearly turned them both to dust. Said they were on the lookout for some runaways and one of them was a Veordya."

"It has to be Liran," Koto muttered, the fear clear in his eyes. "The king sent them here through the teleportation circle."

"Why would he do that?" Zimu asked. "Nobody uses the circle in the Prism Tower anymore."

"They do if you just escaped from the castle dungeons," Koto replied. "And if you maybe murdered the king's right hand advisor."

"And if you're an ex courtesan to the king himself," Ninsar added.

"And, you know, if your old friend is now a king and he wants to kill you and the Sage so he can take over the kingdom with evil dragons and magic." Tyler sighed. "Oh, and he wants to kidnap the friend we're after too and turn him evil as well."

Zimu's eyes grew big as she stared at the three of them, her pipe abandoned. For a long moment she said nothing, taking time to process everything they'd laid on the table all at once. At last she pushed herself up from her chair and walked over to the window, taking another pull from her pipe. She looked up at the dark sky where the stars were shining brightly.

"It seems like you've gotten involved with some pretty serious things," she said. "Rumors have made it here that tell of dragon attacks across the country and that the Sage is behind them."

"That's a lie," Tyler responded, not waiting for the other two. "It's the king who's summoning the dragons, not the Sage. He told me so himself."

"So be it," she nodded. "And other rumors reach my ears that the king is taking on slaves, something the royals abolished centuries ago in the more refined areas of Bramoria." She glanced back at Ninsar. "Your story proves that to be true." Her eyes wandered over them all as she let out a sigh. "If a problematic king now sits on the throne, it will spell disaster for us all. That much we can be certain of. He sends aid to destroyed towns to gain the people's favor, but if what you say is true, he's manipulating everyone and priming them for a war with the Sage. If he succeeds, the people will fight his war for him without any clue they're being tricked." Her gaze turned to Tyler. "You say you're friends with the king. Why don't you stop him?"

Tyler hung his head. "I wish I could but... something's wrong with him. He's not the guy I used to know." He turned away from the rest of them. "Or maybe he is and I just never knew it. He's had a terrible life and I... I never did anything to stop it. I didn't even think I could, so I never tried." The guilt welled up in his chest as he wondered if it was his fault Clay had become the monster he now was. "Now that he has power he'll do anything to keep it. He said so himself. Maybe if I'd been a better friend this wouldn't have happened."

Zimu crossed the room and pulled Tyler into her arms gently. "People make their own decisions, child. Bad experiences aren't permission to be a bad person, everyone has the ability to choose." She pulled him back, staring down into his eyes. "You are not to blame for his choices." She put a finger under his chin. "But maybe you can help set it right."

"How do I do that?"

"Go to the Sage, like you say. Do everything you can to save this king that used to be your friend." Her face darkened as she turned back to Ninsar. "And if you can't... then do what must be done."

Ninsar nodded, but Tyler pushed himself away from Zimu.

"What? What do you mean?"

"There are some people that can't be saved," Zimu replied calmly. "And they must be stopped."

"You want me to kill him?!"

"If it comes to that." Zimu glanced up at Ninsar. "Anyone can do the deed as long as it's done."

"What the fuck?" Tyler looked between them, then at Koto. "Can you believe this?" He pointed a finger at Ninsar. "I thought this was a brothel, not a den of murderers! Killing is wrong!"

Ninsar crossed her arms, stepping up in front of him. "And how many people do you think Clay has killed, huh?" Her voice was full of venom as she glared down at him. "You watched him murder Faus right in front of your eyes! Will you let him do it again?"

"I'm not going to kill my friend!"

"He's not your friend anymore. He's a bloodthirsty tyrant who has killed many by his own hand and hundreds more with his dragons! What about all those people in the outer villages? Their families and friends? His hands are steeped in blood and you would sit here and do nothing about it?"

"But... the Sage," Tyler stammered. "The Sage will take care of it."

"What the fuck do you think he's going to do? Reason with him? Take him on a fucking vacation?" Ninsar paused for a moment. "No! He's going to fucking kill him and put someone else on the throne."

"He wouldn't," Tyler said, shaking his head. "He just needs to send us home, away from Bramoria and Clay will be fine."

"And if he can't?"

Tyler didn't answer.

"What if he goes back to your world and starts killing people there? Will you care about it then?"

Again, no answer.

Ninsar leaned down close to Tyler, her face inches from his. "I understand he's your friend, but if you allow a proven monster to continue to kill people while you sit idly by, you're just as guilty of murder as he is."

Tyler glared at Ninsar, hating her with every fiber of his being because he knew she was right. He'd already accepted long ago that the people in Bramoria were just as real as anyone else. For weeks he'd watched them live, bleed, and die just like anyone from his own world. Taking Clay back home wouldn't make him any less of a murderer, it would just release him from repercussions in Bramoria, if such consequences were even possible to bring against the king himself.

"Okay," he finally managed to say, although it felt like it took all the energy he had. "You're... You're right."

Ninsar's face softened, her eyebrows furrowing together. For the first time she reached out a hand and placed it on his shoulder. "You won't be alone on this journey. Both Koto and I will be at your side.

And if we can figure out how to save him, Tiragan will be too, I'm sure of it."

"You're asking me to kill the man I've had since I was eight years old... I don't think that's something I can do."

"You won't have to," Koto replied, stepping up beside him. "I'll do it myself if need be." He looked over at Ninsar. "But first we need to see if he can be reasoned with. Maybe the Sage can help us with that."

"I'll give him one chance," she growled, holding up a single finger. "One. After that, I'm not holding anything back. Not after the hell that man has put me through in the castle and all the nights I had to put up with him and his wandering hands. Out of everyone here, he's wronged me the most, so don't expect me to pass up the opportunity if it arises."

Tyler's gaze rested on her for a long moment as his stomach turned, the realization of what she meant sinking in. Immediately he felt stupid and ashamed for not understanding her situation earlier. It had never occurred to him that the palace courtesans never had a choice in who they made themselves available to. He'd pushed it from his mind long ago, labeling it as not his problem. But now that he stared at Ninsar and the hatred in her eyes he had to commend her for her patience with him. He'd been defending her assaulter without even thinking about it. His eyes shifted to the floor as a deep sense of shame and hatred toward Clay curled through his guts.

"I'd hoped your return would be filled with more joy, child," Zimu said, pushing herself up from her chair once more. "But it seems you're tangled in the web of fate now and there's nothing I can do to pull you from it." She walked over to Ninsar and pulled her into a hug. "Does this boy mean that much to you?"

Ninsar nodded against her chest.

"Then go save him."

Tyler looked up at Koto, seeing the worry on his face. He wasn't sure who it was directed at, but as Koto continued to stare into his eyes he realized it was for him. Forcing a tiny half smile, Tyler turned away, walking over to the window. The paint was chipping at the edges of the wooden frame exposing the dark wood underneath.

He leaned his forehead against the cool glass, wondering how in the world he was going to save Clay, if that was even possible. And if he couldn't, how he'd ever be able to watch him be killed by another. It was clear that Clay had become a monster, but something in Tyler told him there was a way to save him, that he couldn't give up yet. He hadn't given up on Danny, so why should Clay be any different? Maybe he could be reasoned with if they just had the right leverage, anything that would give them an edge. For a moment he thought of the Divinarae and what Koto had told him about the power contained there being inaccessible. If Clay had found it, maybe Tyler could too and then take it from him somehow. Stripping Clay down to nothing more than a simple human once more might make him see reason. It was half a plan at best with no idea how to reach the Divinarae or what to do once he was there.

Then again, maybe he could make Clay see the error of his ways without power. However, that would never forgive all the terrible things he'd done or the people he'd hurt along the way. But that was outside of his control. The only choice Tyler had was to find the Sage, save Danny, and then hopefully everything would fall into place. It had to. The Sage would know how to save Danny. At least that's what he kept telling himself. In the morning they'd be well rested and on their way once more. Everything was going to be fine.

Tyler felt a sudden deep rumble through the glass that made him pull away. Through the fogged pane of glass a massive dark shape surrounded by smoke passed over the brothel and headed out over the city. The others looked up, their words cut off mid sentence. They came to the window just as he took a step back. A booming roar filled the air as fire rained down on the eastern edge of the town, setting the pristine white houses alight.

Clay knew where they were and he'd sent another dragon.

Thirteen

"By the gods..." Zimu muttered under her breath. "Not here too."

"We have to do something," Tyler said, turning back and heading for the door.

"What are we going to do?" Ninsar called after him. "That's a *dragon*! We don't stand a chance!"

"Last time didn't go very well, Ty," Koto added, glancing down at his still broken arm. "The Sage isn't coming to the rescue this time either."

"Weren't you the ones standing here not five minutes ago telling me that doing nothing was just as bad as causing the destruction yourself?!"

Neither of them answered, their gazes falling to the floor.

"It's our fault that thing is here," he cried, pointing out the window. "Either we need to leave or we need to do something to get rid of it. The Sage destroyed one with his magic, maybe there's other ways to kill this one too."

"I can help with that," Zimu said, clutching the stone around her neck. "I don't know if I'm strong enough, but I'll try."

"You have people to take care of." Ninsar grabbed Zimu by the wrist. "What will happen to them if you don't come back?"

Zimu reached down and patted her cheek lightly. "And where would they work or live if that beast burns the city to the ground? I have their livelihoods to think about, not just my own."

Just as Ninsar opened her mouth to respond, the door burst open and the three courtesans they'd sent to get supplies rushed into the room, their arms still full of goods. All of them looked thoroughly spooked and ready to bolt.

"Lady Zimu!" a strong looking human man cried. "There's some sort of beast attacking the city! It... It looks like a dragon!"

She pulled away from Ninsar, her expression suddenly growing serious. "It is. And I need you three to remain calm." None of them looked any calmer, but she had their attention. "I need you to leave those supplies here and go back downstairs. Inform the customers what is happening and tell the rest of my people to leave the brothel." Her gaze shifted to the man that had addressed her. "Hiran, you know where my farm is on the southeast side of town just outside the city walls. I need you to lead everyone there and get them inside. I'm trusting you to look over them while I try to do something about the dragon."

"Yes ma'am," he replied with a small bow of his head. "But... But what if something happens to you?"

"I said to lead them," she repeated, her expression giving away her full meaning. "Keep them safe in my stead."

"I..." He faltered for a moment. When he found her unmoving he sighed, bowing his head once more. "Yes ma'am."

"Good. Now go. Get everyone out of here as fast as you can. Leave everything behind that can be replaced. Lives are what's important now."

The three of them dropped the supplies near the door and rushed back out into the hallway. Called orders from Hiran echoed down the hall followed by knocking at the other doors in the dormitory, stirring anyone who might be unaware of the situation.

"They're going to need help to get people moving," Zimu said, heading for the door. "Take whatever supplies you need and meet me on the front porch in five minutes."

With that she slipped out of the room, pulling the door closed behind her. For a moment the three of them stared at one another, the reality of the situation slowly sinking in. Tyler glanced down at the mound of supplies that had been brought to them. Fresh leather armor, a new bow for Koto that he couldn't use due to his injury, rope, climbing gear, thick cloaks, and perishables that would help them through the forest if they could find no other sources of food. None of it would help them defend themselves against a dragon, much less defeat it. Stepping forward, Tyler reached down and pulled out the new leather armor, admiring the sheen of its surface and the delicately shaped ridges where the pieces joined together. His last set had been badly damaged by the Toma and the fire, but it wouldn't stand a chance against dragon fire. He had to do something to help though. It wasn't an option to just sit around and let things happen around him anymore. He needed to stop running from his problems or he'd never be able to face Clay.

"So, what's the plan, Ty?" Koto asked, stepping up beside him. "How are we going to stop it?"

Tyler was silent for a moment. "Clay... doesn't want to kill everyone."

"Right," Ninsar spat. "That's a lie."

"No, really. He told me himself." Tyler glanced up at her. "He understands that if he destroys the whole kingdom he'll have nothing to have control over and he's made it known that all he wants is power." He turned to Koto. "Zimu said Liran is here. He's probably Clay's contact that he sent after us. I think if we can draw him out and make him think he's won, he could probably call off the dragon. Correct me if I'm wrong, but this place seems like a pretty big port city. If Clay destroys it, he might cause other issues that he can't fix with soldiers and wagons full of supplies."

"You're right," Koto nodded. "This is the biggest trading port with the other kingdoms far across the ocean. If they think it's unsafe, they won't send any more goods and that could severely injure Bramoria's standing in the world."

"Okay," Ninsar sighed. "So he's not going to destroy the city completely. What do we do to stop him?"

"Zimu can help us get the dragon's attention and take it down. Between the three of us I think we can pull it off. If Liran thinks he's got us corned, the dragon will stop its attack."

"That plan seems like it leaves a lot to chance," Koto replied, shaking his head. "We already went up against a dragon once and it nearly killed us all. They don't stop."

"That was before Clay knew we were here. Now that he does, he'll make sure the dragon spares us."

"How can you be sure?" Ninsar asked.

"I've known Clay for years. If there's one thing he values above anything else, it's his pride. He'll want to kill us himself now that we've escaped and made him look stupid in front of the entire guard." Tyler glanced between the pair of them. "Trust me on this. Clay never turns down an opportunity to make himself look good and if he wants the kingdom to respect him, he'll need to prove himself again."

Koto sighed. "I don't know..."

"No, he's right," Ninsar replied. Tyler looked to her, surprised to have her support. "The king values his reputation above all else. There's a reason he's feared amongst the staff, but the rest of the world sees him as benevolent. He's a master of manipulation. He'll want us back there for a public execution, it's the perfect time to pin the dragon attacks on the Sage publicly and execute us as his accomplices."

There was a long pause between them, the roars of the dragon echoing in the distance.

"Nothing you say is wrong, but I'm still nervous," Koto replied after a moment. He glanced out the window, the bright flashes of flame lighting up his face as his tail twitched behind him. He turned back to Tyler after a few seconds. "I'll follow your lead, Ty." His face softened a bit. "Just try not to get killed."

"None of us will," Tyler said, holding his hand out flat. "We're in this together."

The other two looked at his hand, then to one another.

"Uh... what are you doing?" Ninsar asked, lifting an eyebrow.

"You know..." Tyler flexed his hand. "Everyone puts their hands on top of one another and we all say like 'go team' or something, right?"

He looked at their confused faces. "They do it in all the movies!" He stared for a moment longer with no reaction from either of them. Sheepishly he pulled his hand back. "I thought we were having a moment."

"Okay..." Ninsar reached down and pulled another piece of armor from the pile and began buckling it up. Her brows furrowed as she glanced back up at them. "You two need to get ready! Zimu is waiting for us!"

Koto began pulling pieces out of the pile as well. Tyler sighed to himself. Everything in Bramoria seemed to be like the stories he'd read in books or the video games he'd played. However, for some reason it didn't fit the movie tropes he'd seen, or at least not all the time. He pushed the thought away, it wasn't important. Gathering up his own armor and weapons he was struck by a different comforting thought. For the first time since they'd joined together, it seemed like they were finally working as a team. Even Ninsar seemed to be onboard with his plan, and winning her trust, even momentarily, was an accomplishment.

With all of his armor finally in place, Tyler tied the bag of boundlessness to his belt and glanced down at the strage stone the phoenix had left behind. He didn't want it to get damaged, but leaving it behind when the building could be burnt to the ground seemed like a bad idea. Instead he gathered it up and slung it over his shoulders, feeling the warmth through his armor as it came to rest against his back. It was silly, but for some reason he felt safer with it on, like it was protecting him. He knew the Sage wasn't going to save them this time if things went wrong, but the amethyst stone offered him some semblance of comfort and he'd take anything he could get when facing down a dragon.

Getting everything together took a bit longer than they expected, but after a few minutes of preparation, the group made their way down to the main floor of the bustling brothel and out into the street. People were streaming out of the building behind them, carrying everything they could wrap up quickly and gathering in the street. There they found Zimu shouting instructions to the courtesans to make their way out of the southern gate. As they approached she gave a nod to Hiran who took her place and she broke away from the crowd.

She gave everyone a once over. "You all look fit for war. What do you need me to do?"

Tyler stepped forward, taking the lead for the first time. "We need to draw the dragon away from the city and into the open. Can you get its attention?"

Zimu smiled wide, holding her hand up. The stone around her neck flashed and above her palm an undulating sphere of pinkish energy began to swirl. "I think I can do that."

"Where's the most open place close to town?"

She pointed off to the southwest where the wall opened up to the ocean. "There's a chunk of land there on the edge of the bay. It's nothing but sand and rocks."

Tyler gestured in that direction. "Lead the way."

Zimu glanced back at Ninsar and Koto, nodded her head, and took off across town at a run. Without hesitation the three followed her, the cries of those in the city rising up over the roars of the dragon. The city was large, but thankfully the brothel was situated close to the docks, making their run a short one. Whitewashed houses flew by as they weaved through the trading district and into the wider streets of the port. In the distance Tyler could see the orange glow of the fires started by the dragon. High above it continued to circle, the smoky wings reflecting the firelight from below. Just as they'd expected, it was keeping the attacks focused on the residential districts of the town and putting on a big display without doing much damage. The attack was significantly less vicious than the others they'd seen in smaller towns, proving that the port city was too important to destroy and that it was only meant to draw them out of hiding. The dragon kept mostly to the northern side, flying up and down the wall in search of people fleeing into the Blightwood. Thankfully the majority of the denizens seemed to be heading south, braving open areas in lieu of the dark forest to the north. Tyler wondered why they were avoiding it, but that would be a problem for another day. If they survived that is.

Zimu led them around a corner and onto the wide road lining the bay itself. Their leather boots pounded against the cobblestones as they ran. Koto's injured arm made his gait awkward, but he still managed to keep up with the rest of them. At the end of the road the wall ran all the way to the water, a small archway in the stone exiting the town. There were several guards stationed there, ushering people through. They looked up and saw the four of them approaching. For some reason, Tyler expected the guards to try to stop them. They were wanted people after all and the reason the dragon was attacking. Instead they stepped aside, clearing the way for Zimu and the others to pass through. Just outside the gate, Zimu immediately hooked back toward the bay, heading for the sandy strip of land that existed there. In less than a minute the four of them were standing on a white sand beach trying to catch their breaths.

"Are you ready?" Zimu asked, looking at the three of them.

They all pulled their weapons and steadied themselves, giving her a nod.

"Ready," Tyler replied. "Get his attention."

"No problem."

Zimu's smile widened as she lifted her hand once more. The stone flared into life as another pink sphere erupted above her hand, the air growing hot all around them. Lifting her eyes to the sky she spotted the dragon and reeled her hand back.

"One pissed off dragon, coming right up."

With that she hurled the sphere into the sky. The moment it disconnected from her hand there was a burst of sound as it streaked over the city at an incredible speed like a beam of light. With a bright pink flash it collided with the dragon's ribcage, the thunderous boom reaching them a second later. It faltered in the air for a moment, trying to right itself before it turned its gaze on them and began to dive in their direction.

Fourteen

The earth shuddered as the dragon crashed to the ground in front of them, sand and stone flying in all directions. Tyler pulled his arm down and saw the beast's bright red eyes staring back at them through the smoke that billowed around it. Energy crackled and sparked over its body as it growled, digging its claws further into the sand with a menacing crunch. Zimu already had her hand raised once more, another sphere of pink energy pulsing with power, her hair swirling from the magical wind. Tyler reached a hand up and pulled hers back down, the sphere disappearing as she turned to him.

"It won't have any effect," he said, keeping his eyes fixed on the dragon. "Both Clay and the Sage had to crush it somehow. Is there a way to unravel the magic somehow?"

"There might be." Zimu's voice was less than confident. "But it will take some time. I don't usually do more than run the lights and deal with rowdy customers. It's been many years since I had to fight like this. If you can keep it distracted, I might have a chance."

"Do what you can. We just need to buy time until Liran shows up. Once they've realized the dragon has found its target, they'll be here any minute to try and collect us."

"What do we do until then, Ty?" Koto asked, his tail twitching nervously behind him as he stared at the dragon.

"Keep your distance and try not to get hit." Tyler glanced at Koto and Ninsar, drawing his sword. "Nobody's coming to the rescue this time. It's up to us."

Tyler rushed forward, hoping he was right and the dragon wouldn't full on murder him with the first strike. He closed the distance in a matter of seconds, hefting the sword over his head. With all of his strength he swung it downwards, but the blade passed right through the creature as if it was made of smoke and struck the sand. It was at that moment he remembered how Danny had been hurt so badly during their last encounter. Weapons had no effect on the beast's ethereal form. Glancing up into the dragon's glowing eyes he waited for the strike that would send him flying across the beach.

The dragon growled in his face, the deep rumbling vibration coursing through Tyler's chest. He saw one of the claws lunge forward and squeezed his eyes shut, bracing for impact. To his surprise he merely felt them wrap around his body and squeeze, the blade falling from his hand. Instead of crushing him, the dragon pulled him back toward its body where the smoke coalesced around him like coils. He felt the smoke strangely solidify into tethers like rope, binding his arms and legs down. With a lazy motion the dragon tossed him into the sand. He landed on his side, wriggling to try and free himself from the magical bindings.

"Tyler!" Koto cried, racing after him.

This time the dragon lashed out, the claws missing Koto by a hair's breadth as he jumped backward. Koto slashed back at the creature, but it passed through the claws without harm. Instead of the disinterest it had shown Tyler, the dragon lunged for Koto, going for the kill once more. Tyler felt a sinking feeling in his stomach as he realized his plan had a huge hole in it. Clay didn't want all three of them, he just wanted Tyler.

Thankfully Koto was fast enough to avoid the bite as the dragon's jaws snapped shut only a foot in front of his body, the clash of teeth echoing over the beach. Darting through the sand, he did everything he could to keep the beast's attention and not get killed in the process. Tyler watched on, terrified that one wrong move could cost him his life as he tried to free himself. He didn't notice Ninsar until she kneeled down at his side. She pulled at the dark ropes, trying to break him free, but her hands passed through them without effect. Her dagger did the same, although she managed to cut through his shirt at the same time.

"Clay only wants me," Tyler said, keeping his eyes fixed on the distracted dragon. "You and Koto need to get out of here! The dragon is going to kill you both if you don't!"

"We're not leaving you behind," she growled. "Tiragan would never forgive me."

"He's never gonna forgive me if you two die from my stupid plan!"

She clicked her tongue at him and kept trying to pull at the smoke ropes, her hands continuing to pass through them as if they were nothing. Twice more Tyler watched Koto be nearly bitten in half, each near miss filling his body with dread. He glanced back to Zimu, forcing himself to look away for a split second. The stone around her neck was glowing brightly and her hands were engulfed in a magenta fire as she stared at the dragon, all of her concentration fixed on destroying it. Already a dark sphere was forming above it, pulling in the nearby smoke it gave off. It wasn't until the wings started being yanked back by the growing darkness that the dragon took notice at last. Reaching up it swiped at the sphere, trying to destroy it. Instead the claws passed through and got stuck, the creature crying out in frustration. Slowly Tyler watched as it began to be dragged into the sphere, like a star being swallowed by a black hole.

A smile spread across his face as Ninsar and Koto stopped to watch as well. They were winning somehow. He turned back to Zimu, opening his mouth to cry out his support when he noticed the dark shapes had appeared behind her. Before he got a chance to form the words, the pommel of a sword cracked Zimu in the back of the head and she crumpled to the ground, the mage stone going dark in an instant. The dragon cried out and Tyler whipped his head back around, watching the sphere disappear. However, the damage had been done to the creature's body. Half of a wing was missing and one of its arms was gone up to the elbow joint. Smoke bled from its wounds like ichor as it tried to push itself back to its feet. A familiar voice rang out over the momentary silence.

"If you're quite finished with this little charade, I think it's time you all surrendered."

Tyler felt the bindings around him loosen and fall away, the dragon's magic fading as it struggled and bled. He pushed himself up from the sand, glancing over to where Zimu lay. Standing over her like a hunter posing with a trophy was Liran. Two other Lacerta henchmen held their swords at the ready behind him, confident smiles spread over their faces.

Liran held up a chunk of black obsidian, the stone catching the moonlight. The dragon began to thrash suddenly as its body faded to smoke and was sucked across the beach into the stone. Hot wind blew over them and Tyler lifted his arm to shield his eyes from the kicked up sand. A few seconds later Liran pulled his arm down, the stone now pulsing orange at its core. Tyler looked to Koto, wondering if Liran had always had a mage stone. As if able to read his mind, Koto shook his head. If Liran had been a mage, he would have caught Koto a long time ago. Clay had given him the power to call the dragon in his stead.

"So what? Is your *king* too afraid to come take care of us himself?" Tyler spat, pushing himself up from the sand. "That seems pretty fucking pathetic considering he thinks himself all powerful."

Liran fixed his gaze on Tyler, a wide smile spreading over his face. "Big talk coming from a boy who can barely stand on his own two feet. Tell me, how did my blade feel buried in your gut?"

Tyler opened his mouth to retort, but Koto stepped in front of him. "Enough of this Liran! You've been my shadow for months because a twisted king fed you lies. Are you going to continue being his disposable dog or are you going to see reason?"

"I'm going to kill you and your bitch," Liran replied, his gaze turning to Ninsar. "Then I'm going to take this brat back to the king to be executed." He glanced at Zimu lying on the ground in front of him. "But where's the fourth? The king has *very* special plans for him."

"None of your fucking business!" Ninsar shouted, her knuckles turning white as she gripped her sword.

"What?" Liran chuckled. "Did your sick puppy die on you?"

Tyler reached out and grabbed Ninsar to stop her from rushing them. "No," he called back, not wanting to give Danny away. "He's watching us right now and he's got his sights trained on you. I wonder how good you are at dodging magic, Liran."

The lizard-like man didn't miss a beat. "Your lies are pathetic. We already know he's missing and that you no longer have your mage stone." He kicked at Zimu and Tyler heard Ninsar growl under her breath. "This is the only magic user in the city and it looks like she wasn't much of a threat. Can't say I'm surprised since she's just an old whore."

Tyler tried to think as fast as he could. Liran had the conjured dragon in his hand and he had a feeling it could be released again at any time, fully formed and recovered from the damage Zimu had inflicted upon it. If they tried to fight, they'd be cut down one way or another. And without Zimu, they were trapped. He racked his brain trying to think of anything that could help them. Danny was far away, the Sage was busy tending to him, and his mage stone was trapped with the Zaba inside the bag of boundlessness. He glanced down at the pouch on his belt. Celindra was still in the bag... and she was probably hungry.

"Fine!" Tyler shouted, throwing his sword to the ground and raising his hands. "I surrender!"

"What the *fuck* are you doing?" Ninsar hissed at him.

"I have a plan. Just follow my lead," he whispered out of the corner of his mouth.

"Well, for the first time you're speaking some sense," Liran replied.

"But you have to let my friends go."

"I'm not making any such promises."

Tyler pulled the pouch from his side and held it up. "If you let them go, I'll bring Danny with me."

Liran's eyes fixed on the pouch. "You're telling me he's in there?" He looked back at the other two. "Do you think I'm stupid, boy?"

"Not at all." Tyler pulled the pouch wide and dropped his sword into it, the blade slipping into nothingness in plain sight. "But I do think I have *exactly* what you and the king want."

The smile on Liran's face disappeared in an instant. "Bring it to me!"

"Let my friends go first!"

Liran held up the pulsing stone, the orange light growing brighter in his hand. "If you want them to live through the next five minutes you'll bring me that bag."

Tyler took a few steps forward and glanced back at Koto and Ninsar. "I'm sorry guys. I can't let you get killed. Not for me." He gave them a small wink and turned back to Liran. "Alright, you win! I'll bring it to you."

Slowly he made his way across the beach, the white sand crunching under his boots. He watched as Liran lowered the stone once more, raising his sword in its place. The two behind him kept their eyes fixed on Tyler as he approached, holding the bag out in front of him. He hoped the sword had gotten Celindra's attention. Liran knew he had them cornered and Tyler was sure that he'd kill the others no matter what. Koto warned him there were few in the world as ruthless as the bounty hunter and Tyler knew that's why Clay had hired him. He needed someone who'd get the job done without mercy.

Coming to a stop in front of the hulking figure, Tyler kept his head bowed. He held out the pouch with shaking hands, trying to look as pathetic as possible. "He's... He's in there."

"Why?" Liran snapped, reaching forward and snatching the bag out of Tyler's hands.

"He's been so sick. We needed a place to let him rest. He... He couldn't walk anymore."

"Pah," Liran spat. "Pathetic."

The bounty hunter stuck his blade in the sand and forced the pulsing stone into a pouch at his side. He pulled the bag of boundlessness wide and stared into the void, nothing but darkness staring back at him.

"Where is he?" he growled. "I don't see him."

"He's just inside." Tyler reached hand forward. "I can pull him out if you like."

Liran yanked the bag back and in one fluid motion, kicked Tyler to the ground. "I don't think so!" he cried. "I watched you put your weapon in there! I'll have none of your tricks, boy!"

Turning the bag sideways he glared at Tyler as he stuffed his arm in up to the elbow. He grumbled under his breath as he felt around, trying to find anything to grab onto. His expression grew more frustrated as he found nothing.

"Give me a light you fool!" he snapped at his companions.

Both of the other Lacerta reached into their pockets, both of them producing a glowing stone and holding them out to Liran. He snatched one with a growl and both of them backed up, clearly terrified of their own leader. Glancing to Tyler, he spit in his direction and pulled the bag wider before stuffing both his arm and head into the opening, the light held in his hand. Tyler watched for a moment as the bounty hunter searched. It wasn't until his body suddenly stiffened that he knew his plan had worked.

All at once Liran began to struggle, trying to pull himself free of the bag. His muffled screams echoed from within as he body was slowly dragged further in. The other two Lacerta glanced at one another, concerned but not sure what to do. Tyler however, didn't waste a second. Springing forward he kicked Liran's legs out from underneath him, the massive body hitting the sand hard. Reaching down he pulled the sword from the sand and cut the pouch with the dragon stone free from Liran's belt, slicing through the scaled flesh at the same time. There was another scream from within the bag and suddenly his body was yanked inward and out of sight.

By the time Tyler looked up at the other two bounty hunters, both Ninsar and Koto were at his side, their weapons leveled. The hunters hesitated, readying themselves to fight. One last blood curdling scream echoed from the bag followed by a sickening snap and there was silence. The two looked at one another, their eyes growing wide. Without hesitation they both threw down their weapons at Tyler's feet, not wishing to meet the same fate as their leader.

A rush of endorphins filled Tyler's body as he stood there staring them down. For the first time since he stepped foot in Bramoria, the feeling of victory washed over him. Reaching down he grabbed the bag with the dragon stone inside of it. Tipping it over he let the stone fall into his open palm. The orange glow still radiated from within the dark smoky depths. He turned it over, looking at it from all sides. For a moment he wondered if he could use it again, but as he stared he saw the light go out. With a sharp crack the stone split, the two halves crumbling to dust in his hand.

Fifteen

It felt strange to leave the brothel after being there for two days, but Tyler knew they'd already stayed too long. Danny was waiting for them on the other side of the Blightwood forest and it was time they got started. Zimu, after coming back to consciousness, had given them a place to recover after the events of the dragon attack. With her help they'd managed to have the remaining bounty hunters arrested by the guard. Nobody was sure how long their imprisonment would last, but it would at least keep them out of the way until the trio could get clear of Zoethaven. Liran, on the other hand, was assumed dead and consumed. Tyler had opened the bag once and called for him into the void. All he heard was a low rumbling laugh from Celindra and a tone of surprise to hear he was still alive.

With his things packed and most of his aches healed, Tyler waited on the front porch of the Gilded Clam for his companions. The porch was mostly deserted early in the morning, although a few die hard patrons were already inside getting their daily dose of ale and titillation. Leaning against the railing he looked out over the city that was still shrouded in mist blown in from the ocean. The first beams of light from the rising sun caught the tower and the crystal prism at its peak. The moment it struck the center of the stone a rainbow of colors spilled down on the misty city, the fog blending them together to create even more radiance.

Tyler stared as if lost in a dream. There were moments where he found himself wishing he never had to leave Bramoria. His problems melted away and he could get lost in the beauty of the world around him that was so unlike his own. In those moments there were no parents to please, no one to save, and no harsh realities to deal with. It was just him and the beating of his own heart. Those fleeting minutes of silence made him yearn for more. In the safety of his own mind he was able to admit he'd been lying to himself and his friends about wanting to go home for some time. Even so, he found it hard to imagine living out the rest of his life inside of a storybook. Besides, the hero never got to stay, that's how it always went. He didn't consider himself a hero, but he figured the same rules applied to anyone sucked into a magic book and there was no reason to believe this one was any different.

"It's beautiful, isn't it?"

Tyler glanced over his shoulder to see Ninsar drop her bag and step up beside him. She leaned over the railing and craned her head up to the sky, watching the rainbow of colors dance over the city as the prism shimmered.

"This was always my favorite part of living here," she continued. "It's the reason I stayed for so long. That... and what I mistook for love."

"What happened?"

"The same thing that always happens," she sighed, her words flowing easily. "A sweet man came to town and he took an interest in me. He said everything I wanted to hear, respected me, and earned my trust." She shook her head, dropping her gaze back to the ground. "And then after he fucked me he turned me in for the bounty money."

"I... I'm sorry," Tyler replied, not really sure what to say. "That sounds awful."

"It's no different than most men that come to a brothel, but I should have known better. I was too naive and in love to see the signs right in front of my nose." She huffed and looked back up at the prism. "And I paid for it many times over."

"It sounds dangerous," Tyler said absentmindedly. "To fall in love I mean."

"It can be," she nodded. "But it can also be the most amazing thing to ever happen to someone."

"Is that how you feel about D– Tiragan?"

There was a long pause. "I... I don't know. I haven't known him that long, but he's a genuinely nice person... or at least he seems that way." She glanced over at Tyler. "Did you know we just sat up talking that night at the castle? He told me about his life, about all the things he's dealt with and being sick. It seemed like he had an entire life worth of dreams and fears that he'd bottled up. At first I thought he was just some pathetic boy, but as he continued to speak I started to like him. It wasn't until you walked in on us that things started to progress any further." Ninsar shrugged her shoulders. "I'm not sure why I'm telling you all this."

"Tiragan is a good guy," Tyler said, ignoring her last comment. "I've known him all my life and he's always been wonderful even though his life has been so hard. His parents are the richest people in town and don't get me wrong, but having money doesn't count for much when you're too sick to even leave your room." Tyler hung his head. "It scared me so much to watch him wither away in front of me. I haven't seen him much in the past few months because I couldn't stand to watch him slowly die. Then when I finally came to see him my worst fears were confirmed. He wasn't going to live past the end of summer." He lifted his gaze to Ninsar. "Did you know it was me that suggested we run away? I told myself I did it for him, but really I was trying to make myself feel less guilty for abandoning him." He gestured out to the city around him. "And now look what I've got him all mixed up in."

"He talked about you a lot, you know," she replied. "He told me how you'd made his life much better, that you'd always been the best friend he ever had. I think he was scared he'd run you off when you didn't visit, but he didn't hold it against you. There were moments where it slipped through, but for the most part he understood."

"But now he's going to die in this world, away from everyone he knows and it's all my fault."

Ninsar reached out and placed her hand on his arm. "Either you don't understand or you refuse to see the truth." Her tone was more serious, but not unkind. "Tiragan is eternally grateful to you for taking him on that trip. If you hadn't, he never would have ended up in Bramoria, the place of his dreams. And..." She paused for a moment. "And I'm grateful too. Without you, I never would have met him."

Tyler looked up to meet her gaze, noticing the tears forming at the corners of her eyes.

"It might seem unfair, but he's happy here. Even if it's only for a short while. This was something he wanted more than anything and it's thanks to you he got it before it was too late."

"I... I don't want him to die."

"Neither do I," she said, reaching up to wipe her eyes. "And that's why we're going to go to the Sage and find a way to save him." Her voice shifted to one of determination. "If he's half as good as I think he is, he deserves to live."

"He's the best person I've ever known."

"Then we have to try. For his sake and that of Bramoria. With someone like that on our side, we might be able to stop the king once and for all."

Tyler smiled for a moment, feeling the confidence in her voice course through him. But a second later it faded as he realized what she meant. "So I have to kill one friend to save the other," he murmured, leaning further over the railing to stare at the dirt. "It seems no matter what I do, someone important to me is going to die." He sighed, thinking of his mother. "And maybe more if I can't figure it out fast enough."

"I don't want you to think I'm heartless," Ninsar replied, putting her arms back on the railing. "But I don't see any other way to stop him. The king is ruthless. You've seen it with your own eyes."

"I just don't understand what happened to him. He's had a bad life, but even that seems like a poor excuse for what he's become. I wish... I wish I had done more to help him but I don't know what I could have done." He looked up at Ninsar, feeling more pathetic than ever. "My mom struggled to keep a house over our heads and food on the table. If I'd offered to have him live with us it would have been more of a burden on her and I couldn't do that. Not to mention his piece of shit dad might have broken down our door to get him back if I'd tried. I'm not even considered an adult in my world yet..." He tore his gaze away from her, the feeling churning in his chest. "But even all that is just an excuse. The real reason I didn't help him... is because I was scared. I was scared of losing Clay just like I was scared of losing Danny. Both of them are so much smarter than me, but I was the only one having a semi-normal life. I was worried that if things got better for them, I'd be left all alone again."

"Again?"

"My dad ran off when I was a kid and my mom works all the time." He shrugged. "I don't blame her for it, but Clay and Danny are my only friends. It's pathetic, but they're all I have." Tyler's eyes widened as he glanced at Ninsar. "Fuck... I meant Tiragan. I'm sorry." He kicked at the railing on the porch, the wood creaking against his boot. "Even in this made up world I'm still such a fuck up. I can't even get his name right."

"Change takes time," she said matter of factly. "Even Tiragan realizes that. He's not asking you to be perfect, just for you to accept him as he's accepted you and try your best." She turned around and leaned her back against the railing with her arms crossed. "As for the rest of it, I think Tiragan was right. You put a lot of energy into trying to make everyone else happy and yet you do almost nothing for yourself." She glanced over, her eyes boring into his. "Don't you think you've spent enough time wallowing in self pity?"

Tyler's skin prickled and his brows furrowed together. "You know, sometimes I think you and I are getting somewhere and then you go and say shitty things like that."

"Then maybe it's the shitty things you need to hear," she replied unapologetically. "You're so busy sitting here feeling sorry for yourself and making excuses that you don't have time to actually try to make things better. If you stopped throwing a pity party for a moment you might realize that you are the only person in the whole world who has the power to change your own life." She leaned in close, her eyes narrowing. "But you have to *want* it."

"I *do* want it," he sniped back.

"Then fucking work for it." She stared at him for a long moment, the tension between them nearly causing sparks in the air. "You can sit here wanting and wishing all day long about the past and nothing will ever change." She lifted a hand, her finger pointing out toward the rising sun through the mist. "But if you go out into the world and actually *try*, you'll find you can't help but make some progress even if you fail. You don't always get what you want, but at least you won't be wallowing in your own misery with nothing to show for it but a lot of whiny sentiment."

Tyler stared at her, feeling the heat rising in his neck. He wanted to scream, to yell at her and tell her how stupid and wrong she was. But he couldn't bring himself to form the words. Not because he didn't have the ability, but because he knew she was right. He'd been doing exactly what she'd accused him of. For years he'd done everything in his power to please everyone but himself, and avoided those situations that would cause too much change in his world. College had terrified him and for the first time he truly understood why. He'd been trying to preserve the delicate balance of his childhood indefinitely. It wasn't the book or Bramoria that had brought it crashing down around him, but time itself. He was growing up and adulthood just around the corner terrified him. And with it came hard decisions that he didn't know if he was prepared to make.

"What do I do?" Tyler whispered. "I... I've never done this before."

Ninsar reached out and took his hand, placing it on the pommel of his sword. "You fight." She pointed again toward the horizon. "You go out there and you live your own truth, fight for what you believe in, and don't give up even if it kills you."

Tyler felt a hand on his shoulder. "And we'll be there beside you, if you'll have us." Koto stepped up beside him, a smile on his face. "Not that you could get rid of me at this point."

"You guys don't have to do this," Tyler replied, reaching up to wipe away the tears threatening his cheeks. "But I... I need your help to save Tiragan. And Clay if we can."

Ninsar held out her hand, palm facing the ground. "Then we're in this together."

Koto placed his on top of hers. "Till the end."

Tyler followed suit, staring at their hands all resting on top of one another.

"We're having a moment aren't we?" he sniffled, glancing up at the other two as a single tear rolled down his cheek. "It's like we're in a nineties movie."

Sixteen

The Blightwood forest was a lot less terrifying than Tyler expected. They'd already been traveling its depths for a day and nothing seemed out of place. In fact, it reminded him a lot of the state parks back home. The trees were tall, their canopies blocking out most of the light while the forest floor was nothing but leaf litter and small plants that thrived in the shade. Here and there they ran across a rabbit or a family of squirrels, but beyond that it was as pleasant of a place as he could imagine.

"So what's the deal with this place?" he finally asked as the afternoon began to wane on their second day. "Why does everyone avoid it like the plague?"

"There's more than a few strange things in these woods," Ninsar responded. "I heard about a couple of them when I was living in Zoethaven, although I've never seen them for myself."

"What kinds of things?"

"Typical stuff like monsters, werewolves, and things of that nature." She shrugged as if it was nothing. Tyler had to stop himself from asking about the werewolves. "But the Blightwood got its name from the giant fungi that grow deep in the forest. They have a tendency to infect animals and plants alike, spreading their toxic spores across the region."

Tyler froze up, glancing around for any signs of the murder mushrooms. "We're not going there, right?"

"We'll have to pass close by to get to the Sage," Koto replied. "But I've been through once before with the king. There is a path."

"At one time the mushrooms had nearly reached the edge of Zoethaven," Ninsar continued. "That's why the walls were built, to keep out any infected animals or people. But it's been decades since the fungi have gotten that close again." She glanced back at Koto. "What path are you talking about?"

"The Obsidian Road," he replied quietly.

Ninsar stopped dead in her tracks, turning on her heel to stare at him. "Are you completely fucking crazy?! We'll be burned alive before we travel even half a mile!"

"I'm afraid to ask..." Tyler began.

"The Obsidian Road is along the edge of the only volcano in the Dravin Peaks. It's called that because the path literally erupts into fire sometimes as the hot air and molten glass escapes the trapped magma below. Not to mention the entire road is nothing but broken glass shards."

"You have got to be kidding me," he said, shaking his head in disbelief. "A path that erupts in fire constantly? The next thing you're going to tell me is that the woods are full of rodents of unusual size."

"How do you know about the Toma?" Koto said, his brows furrowed in confusion.

"Oh my fucking god... I'm living in *The Princess Bride*."

"What princess? Did she tell you about the Toma?"

"Nevermind," Tyler replied, waving him off. He looked at Ninsar. "Can you please tell me what we're up against here?"

"I won't have to." She pointed across the forest toward a series of dark stones jutting up out of the forest floor. "We're almost to the base of the volcano."

THEY DECIDED TO BED down for the night before pressing forward. Both Ninsar and Koto seemed reluctant to go much further without the light of day to guide them. Tyler couldn't blame them. Between killer mushrooms, giant rodents, werewolves, and fire breathing pathways, it sounded like something he'd rather avoid all together. Even the thought of crossing just the mountains was exhausting, much less all the other nonsense in between. But as much as he wanted to run away or give up, he knew the Sage was waiting for them and Danny was running out of time fast. If he wanted to have any chance of saving his friend, they'd need to get through the forest and over the mountains quickly.

In the early morning they headed for the stones jutting out of the forest floor that Ninsar had pointed out the day before. At first Tyler wasn't sure how they'd gotten there. They seemed to suddenly appear out of nowhere at first, but as the canopy overhead began to break up, he could at last see the black mountain rising up in front of them. It rose to a jagged broken peak, evidence of an eruption that had taken place long ago. It wasn't until then he noticed the angle at which all the stones had impacted the ground. They'd come from the top of the mountain.

His eyes scanned over the volcano. Here and there a scrubby bush clung to the sheer face of a cliff, barely able to survive such a harsh landscape. The warm wind picked up immediately and Tyler caught the smell of sulfur on the breeze. Koto and Ninsar hadn't been lying, the volcano was still active. He craned his neck, trying to get a better look through the trees. Every now and then he caught sight of a thin trail of black smoke, part of the path they were heading for he assumed.

It took another half hour to reach the base of the mountain where the trees finally gave way to the black rock and loose soil. Tyler craned his neck back, trying to take in the sheer magnitude of the monolith that stood before him. He'd never seen anything like it in his life.

"We're going to climb this thing?" he asked, looking at the other two. "Are we sure the mushrooms are that dangerous?"

"Trust me," Ninsar replied. "If you saw a creature infected by them, you wouldn't be asking that question." She pointed across the way to a swath of slowly rising ground switchbacking up the mountain. "That's where we start. The Obsidian Road is waiting for us at the top."

"Why go up so high?" Tyler shielded his eyes, trying to get a better look at where they were headed. All he could make out were thin trails of black smoke. "Couldn't we just go above the treeline?"

"We have to get high above the trees to avoid contamination." Ninsar seemed to be growing tired of his questions. "The wind carries the spores and we'll be passing by the worst of it directly." She lifted an eyebrow in his direction. "A little hiking won't kill you. You're too damn skinny anyway."

Tyler turned to Koto as Ninsar walked away. "I thought I was getting better?" He looked himself over. "I look more muscular already."

Koto smiled, placing a hand on his shoulder. "You've only been here for three weeks." He hesitated for a moment. "You... still look the same to me."

Tyler huffed. "Fine, okay. But have I been complaining as much?"

"Yes!" Ninsar called from ahead of them.

"Not you, smartass!" Tyler cried back. "Nobody asked you!" He turned back to Koto. "Am I really that bad?"

"Not at all," Koto chuckled. "In fact, I think you've improved a lot in just a short time. I remember when you didn't want to get involved in anything and you thought this whole world was just a dream."

"Sometimes I still do," he admitted. "And don't count me as a good guy yet. I know you want to help the people in this world, but I really only want to save Da– Tiragan."

"That's still helping people, Ty," Koto nodded. He reached up and put his hand around Tyler's shoulders, pulling him forward to catch up with Ninsar. "You might be focusing on one person, but you'll be helping a lot more if you also take care of the king."

"You mean if I kill him."

Koto didn't reply.

"Do you regret killing your father?"

The hand slipped off his shoulder as Koto stopped, his eyes distant at the unexpected question. He paused for a moment, his tail twitching. "Sometimes I do," he finally said. "I wish that I could have saved him. Made him see reason. Even though the prince used magic to switch places with him, I know in my heart that I would have had to kill him eventually." He looked back up at Tyler. "Ninsar was right. You can't let evil exist in the world just because it's hard to get rid of. Sometimes the only answer is violence."

Tyler sighed. "Everything I was ever taught growing up would contradict that sentiment. Everybody is always saying 'violence isn't the answer'..." He waved for Koto to keep walking with him. "But I've read too many stories and seen too many things in my own world that would prove you right. There are people out there that do nothing but cause harm. I'm not sure if it's right to kill them, but I know it's wrong to let them continue to hurt people." He paused for a moment. "I wish I had understood that when Clay came to me for help after his dad beat him up. Or every time I joked about him coming to live with me, but didn't mean it. Maybe then I could have saved him, could have stopped him from becoming the monster he is now." Tyler kicked at a rock, sending it skittering across the path. "If I go through with it, I just wonder how I'll ever forgive myself."

"Maybe you won't have to do it." Koto's ears flattened against his head as he rubbed his slung arm nervously. "I... I could do it for you. There's already plenty of blood on my hands."

"Why?" Tyler stopped. "Why would you do that for me?"

"Because I–"

"Koto! Tyler!" Ninsar yelled from up ahead. "Run!"

"I swear to god... she is the most annoying person I've ever met in my life." He looked up at Koto expecting a smile, but there was only fear on his face. "What's wrong?"

Following Koto's gaze he turned on his heel, glancing back toward the forest. Standing at the edge of the treeline were several small hunched figures cast in shadow. He squinted, trying to make out what they were, but their shapes didn't make sense. They were moving toward him, their gait stumbling and irregular, almost like they were zombies in a bad horror movie.

But as the first stepped into the light, Tyler felt the breath catch in his throat. They were humanoid and no more than four feet tall with spindly limbs and ropey muscles. Their faces were elongated like rats with bulging black eyes and a mouth full of sharp yellow teeth. Fur covered most of their bodies and a thin piece of cloth was tied around their waists. To Tyler they almost looked like a goblin had been crossed with a rat. Or at least that's what they would have looked like if not for the missing patches of fur, dark bloody scabs, and clear liquid oozing out of every visible orifice. Out of wounds, eyeballs, and ears, mushrooms sprouted. Most were bright orange with thin stems and a delicate honeycomb texture. As the creatures moved, puffs of spores erupted from the mushrooms, filling the air around them with a whitish haze. Tyler's eyes fell to the rusted swords and makeshift spears held at their sides.

"Are those... the Toma?" he whispered.

"And the Blight of the forest," Koto replied. "It must be spreading again."

"Run you fucking idiots!" Ninsar yelled again.

A shrill cry rose up from the Toma as her words echoed over them. All at once the stumbling creatures broke into a sprint with their weapons held high. Tyler felt his heart pounding in his throat. They had their eyes set on him and Koto.

Seventeen

Tyler ran as hard and fast as he could, the Toma hot on his trail. Koto was a few feet ahead and Ninsar was already on the mountain path, waving for them to hurry up. Stealing a glance behind him, he was relieved to see the Toma had fallen behind. Their tiny legs and mutilated bodies had slowed them down enough to give Tyler and his companions a sizable lead.

Ahead Ninsar was already several feet off the ground standing at the edge of a small cliff. Not wanting to take the extra time to go around, Koto and Tyler both took a flying leap, latching onto the stone. Koto was up and over in a flash before turning back to help Tyler up behind him. The Toma's shrill hoarse cries echoed over the mountainside, making his blood run cold.

"Run you idiots!" Ninsar yelled, grabbing both of them by the shirt and pulling them forward. "If we inhale those spores we'll be as good as dead!"

One of the Toma collided with the small cliff at their feet, a cloud of white spores rising up from their body. Without hesitation all three of them clamped their mouths shut and took off up the side of the mountain. The path was covered with loose dirt and black stones, causing Tyler to nearly faceplant more than once. Koto stayed at his side, faithfully catching him every time he tripped.

Ninsar took the lead, pushing them further and further up the mountain. It was only a matter of minutes before Tyler's legs were almost numb and the burning in his lungs was nearly unbearable, yet on they ran. The path switched back and forth, taking them ever higher above the forest canopy. Steep hillsides fell away at either side, one false move and they'd tumble all the way down. The likelihood of surviving the fall was good, but not so unscathed as to run away from the Toma waiting to tear them apart. Their screams were the only thing that kept Tyler going until he was barely moving faster than a walk.

"We have... to do... something," he puffed, his legs dragging over the ground like lead. "I can't... keep going... like this."

Ninsar stopped, a look of irritation on her face. "If you want to live, you'll keep running!"

"Ninsar, please," Koto said, taking his side. "He's nearly fallen off the side of the mountain three times already. And I'm... I'm tired too. We can't keep this up forever." He pointed up the mountainside to the trails of black smoke. "The path isn't that far away and we've got a good lead. Let's just move a little slower for a few minutes." He fixed his gaze on her. "For *all* our sakes. I know you want to save Tiragan, but we can't rush this and get clumsy. If we die here it will all be for nothing anyway."

"Fine," she huffed, trotting back down to them. "You have one minute and that's it."

Tyler slumped down to the ground as he watched her step up to the edge of the path. Bending down she picked up a bowling ball sized rock and held it over her head, staring at the path below. When the Toma came into her line of sight she hurled it downward. For a long moment there was no sound, then a sudden shrill screeching and the crashing of other things, possibly bodies, as they tumbled down the mountain. It seemed she'd hit her target, although Tyler wasn't sure where she was getting all the energy from. She was even skinnier than him, but she had more endurance than both him and Koto put together.

Koto pulled out a wine skin full of water and handed it to him. "Are you doing alright?"

Tyler sat there with his legs shaking, still trying to catch his breath. "I'm okay I guess." He took a deep draught from the wine skin. "How much further is it?"

"We're only about halfway up the mountain," Koto replied, his expression filled with worry. "The Obsidian Road is about two thirds of the way up. It's not too much further, but we'll need to be on our guard once we step foot there. Every inch of that path is filled with danger and one false move means you're toast."

"Great," Tyler sighed, taking another drink. "I'm looking forward to it." He glanced over the edge of the cliff, looking down at the scattered Toma that were screaming at one another in some strange beastial language. "You know, this would all be a lot easier if there wasn't something trying to kill us every other day." He glanced back up at Koto. "Please tell me it gets easier."

"I have a feeling we're being actively targeted," Koto replied, his ears pinning to his head. "I think your friend wants us dead more than any of us anticipated. Toma that infected can barely walk, much less track and hunt down prey. Someone sent them straight to us."

"Why though?" Tyler asked, the irritation filling his voice. "He's got all this power and he's the leader of a whole country! I mean, yeah I found his book and all his dastardly plans and I'll probably tell them to the Sage so he can..." Tyler glanced back at Koto. "Okay, fine. I see your point."

"I knew you'd figure it out eventually," Koto laughed, trying to keep their conversation as light hearted as possible. "You're unlike any other person I've ever met."

"Are you calling me stupid?"

"Not at all. A little strange, but nothing more." He held out a hand to help Tyler back to his feet. "I think our minute is almost up."

"It's been up," Ninsar grumbled, kicking another large rock over the edge of the path. "And those rats are keeping close to the cliff now. Bastards." She made her way ahead of the group. "Let's go."

Tyler glanced up at Koto, noticing the man's eyes flick away for a moment, as if he didn't want to be seen staring at him.

"As long as we're walking, I can keep up I think," he said, reaching out and taking Koto's hand to help him up.

"It better be a fast walk!" Ninsar called back, nearly to the next bend in the path already.

As Koto pulled Tyler to his feet he felt his legs give out for a second and fell into him, his hands catching Koto's armor. Looking up he saw the sea green eyes staring down at him and immediately felt his face flush.

"S-Sorry," he mumbled, righting himself as quickly as possible. His heart was pounding in his chest and he didn't understand why. It must have been the adrenaline of being pursued by the Toma.

"Don't worry about it," Koto said, a smirk pulling at his lips as he gave Tyler a once over. "Come on, let's catch up with Ninsar."

"Yep. Right. Good idea."

A HALF HOUR LATER AND in more pain than he'd been in since he was stabbed, Tyler found himself standing at the edge of a smoking pathway. Near the top of the mountain there was a shelf of rock at least twenty feet wide that seemed to have been cut away in the past explosion of the volcano. Rising pillars of smoke and steam dotted the shelf, the glow of magma peaking through in some places. The air stunk of sulfur and the path was covered in a carpet of broken shards of obsidian glass. Every minute or two a plume of fire would erupt out of the ground in a random spot. Unlike the movies he'd seen, these ones didn't come with an auditory warning.

"Stay close behind me and follow my path exactly," Ninsar said, stepping out onto the path.

"Have you been here before?" Tyler asked, watching her with trepidation.

She paused for a moment. "No."

"Then how the fu–" He took a deep breath to calm himself and turned to Koto. "I'm not trying to be insensitive... but you have ears... can you... ya know..."

"Sense something you humans can't?"

"Yeah," Tyler exhaled, glad to have avoided offending him. "Yeah that."

"Voerdya do have more heightened senses." Koto stepped out in front of Ninsar. "Let me go first. I've got the best chance of knowing an eruption is coming." He glanced at the other two. "And a better chance of avoiding one."

"Just be quick about it," she huffed, glancing back over the side of the mountain. "Those Toma aren't far behind and I don't feel like becoming a human mushroom today."

"Yes ma'am."

"Koto!" Tyler called, unable to help himself. The man looked over his shoulder, his tail unmoving. "Don't... Just be careful."

He gave a small smile and a nod before turning back to the obsidian strewn path in front of him. Tyler sighed, not knowing what had come over him. His heart was beating too quickly and he felt his face flushing once more. He was starting to wonder if he was coming down with something or if he'd gotten a mouthful of those mushroom spores without realizing it. Shaking his head he noticed Ninsar staring at him. She lifted a single eyebrow, then turned away, muttering something under her breath. He didn't understand what she was annoyed about now, but as another screech echoed over the mountain from the Toma, he decided he didn't care and fell in step with her.

At first Tyler thought the fire would be the most dangerous part of the path, but he soon realized it was actually the obsidian glass. The piles of shards were not only razor sharp, but they rolled under his boots with every step like marbles. After hiking up an entire mountain, his legs were already like jello, but the glass made it even harder to keep his feet under him. With every step he felt the shards dig into the thick leather. The boots were practically brand new having been purchased in Zoethaven, but he knew after their short trip over the glass they'd be nothing but shreds. Chunks of leather were peeling away with every passing step.

Ninsar slipped in front of him, pulling him from his thoughts in a flash. He was able to catch her elbow at the last second, stopping her from hitting the ground with her bare hands. He pulled her back to her feet, waiting until she was steady to let go.

"Thanks," she muttered, her tone genuine. Koto had stopped a few feet ahead and was staring back at them. "Do you think we should wrap our hands?"

"I don't think you're going to have time," he said, pointing behind them, his ears flat against his head.

Tyler turned around and saw the Toma already finding their way to the edge of the path. Several had broken mushrooms or dislocated limbs from the stones pushed down the mountain by Ninsar. One of them was even missing a hand completely, the stump oozing blood that looked far too thick to be healthy. Their cries rose up as Tyler and his companions noticed them, sending a shiver down his spine. He'd thought they were lifeless zombies, but it seemed they still retained some intelligence. The Toma were hunting them, trying to sneak up on their prey without being found out. Recalling some of the things he'd learned about certain mushrooms in biology, he was wondering if the Toma were in control of their bodies or if the fungus was directing them to trying to find a new host.

The first of the Toma took a step out onto the obsidian shards. For a moment Tyler thought they wouldn't feel the pain of the glass because of the fungi, but it was merely a delayed reaction. The Toma screamed out a moment after the shards crunched under its weight, easily tearing through the half rotted flesh. However, instead of backtracking, it took another step, and then another. It was a horrifying display to watch a still living creature was forced to put itself through unbearable pain with no way to fight against it, the cries of agony echoing across the mountainside. The sight sickened him, but he didn't have time to dwell on it, especially with the mushroom spores already gathering in a small cloud around the ugly creatures.

"We need to move faster," he said as he watched the other Toma follow suit, each of them taking their first steps onto the Obsidian Road. "They're not stopping."

"I was afraid of that," he heard Ninsar mutter under her breath. "Pick up the pace, Koto!"

The Veordya shook himself from his stupor and turned back to the path. Without choosing his steps too carefully, he continued to lead them down the road. Here and there he steered clear of open vents that were still glowing white hot inside, a trail of smoke and stinking air crawling up from under the ground. Through his boots Tyler could feel the heat of the magma below the surface. He wondered how far down it was and how little stone separated them from an agonizing death. His heart was already pounding in his chest, every step and thought filling his head with anxiety. Each of his senses were on high alert, looking for any tiny signal that he was in danger of a sudden burst of flame. However, nothing warned him when the explosion finally came. A plume of fire shot into the air some five feet behind Tyler, the heat washing across his body in an instant, curling the hairs on his head.

"Holy fuck!" he cried, jumping back against Ninsar and Koto, nearly knocking them over. It took him a moment to right himself, readjusting the pack that held the phoenix stone on his back. "Sorry," he muttered to the other two, feeling foolish for his overreaction. The heat was intense, but it hadn't been close enough to burn him. "Okay," he murmured to himself and took a deep breath. "Stay calm. We're gonna be fine."

Koto opened his mouth to respond, but his gaze stopped over Tyler's shoulder. Tyler's heart sank as he looked back to see the Toma only a dozen feet away, their bloody feet stuck full of obsidian shards. Their cries had grown raspy and guttural, like the heat and glass were wearing them down, but they still didn't stop. In fact, now that they were so close, it seemed their energy was returning, the cloud of spores thickening around them.

"Run!" Ninsar cried, grabbing at the pair of them before she took off.

All three of them dug into the glass, trying to put as much distance between them and the Toma as possible. He could hear the muffled cries of the beasts as they drew closer. It seemed like they were right on his heels. Ninsar and Koto were faster than Tyler and he could see them slowly getting further and further ahead. The climb up the mountain had made his legs useless and although the adrenaline helped propel him forward, it was quickly running out. With each step he felt his knees and calves grow weaker and he knew one false move would lead to a faceful of glass. Behind him the raspy cries were nearly at his ankles and it became obvious he wasn't going to outrun them.

With a split second decision, Tyler pulled his sword from its sheath. He dug his heels into the obsidian and skidded to a stop, turning to face the Toma. Taking a deep breath, Tyler forced his lips shut and his tongue to the roof of his mouth. Behind him he heard both Koto and Ninsar cry out, but he wasn't listening anymore. The next few seconds were all that stood between him and death. Reeling his sword back, he prepared to intercept the first Toma.

A shocked expression crossed the creature's face the moment before Tyler swung his sword like a baseball bat, severing the head from its shoulders in one swipe. He watched as the head fell to the ground, the face instantly stuck full of obsidian shards and dark viscous blood oozing out of its stump of a neck and rolled over the edge of the path, careening down the mountain. A cloud of spores erupted from the mushrooms attached to the creature as if they could sense their imminent death at the loss of their host. Tyler had but a moment to feel the revulsion swell in his stomach before two more Toma were nearly on top of him.

Still holding the breath tight within his chest, he lashed out at the first Toma. His blade quickly sliced through a few of the mushrooms on its shoulders before burying itself in the beast's clavicle. Tyler felt the sickening crunch of metal on bone and he had to yank the sword free before the creature slumped to the ground. However, the other took the momentary distraction to lash out at him with his rusted and chipped blade. Seeing it coming, Tyler ducked to the side, the sword just catching on the strap of his bag. He felt the blade tear through and the other slipped from his shoulder. The phoenix stone clattered to the ground with a dull ring against the glass, the sound melodic and strangely soothing. He wanted to reach for it, but he only had a moment to lift his blade once more to block the Toma from landing a secondary blow. With a quick thrust he drove his sword through the Toma's chest, gave it a twist like Koto had taught him, and pulled it free. The creature fell forward onto the obsidian as blood gushed from his now open chest.

Tyler's lungs were burning as he looked up, at least half a dozen more Toma rushing his way, their blades drawn and reared back to strike. The cloud of spores around him was already thick and he wondered what would happen if they got into an open wound should one of their blows land. The dust was already gathering on his clothing, meaning his friends could no longer get close to him. From behind he could hear the shouts of Koto and Ninsar telling him to run for his life, but his legs wouldn't listen. He could barely stand as it was and the exhaustion was close to overtaking him. As he looked on at the creatures only a few feet away he realized he didn't have time to run even if he could. There was nothing to do but stand and fight. Tyler shifted his stance wider, trying to give himself a better foundation. He glanced up too late and realized it wouldn't matter as three swords came his way all at once.

Suddenly there was a loud crack and the ground under his feet shifted. A rush of hot air washed across him, driving the mushroom spores away. The Toma skid to a halt, their blades dropping to their sides as plumes of flame erupted all around them. Tyler threw his arms up to shield his eyes, feeling the ground continue to rock and shift. It wasn't until he heard the rushing of obsidian glass, like a heavy rain, and felt a blast of heat that he looked down. The ground had split open to his right, a bright orange glow pouring out. He watched as the phoenix stone rocked on the edge of the newly formed crevasse and tipped forward. Tyler tried to reach for it, but it was too late. The stone rocked forward and fell into the liquid magma pooling just below the surface.

Again the ground shifted and Tyler felt his feet sliding across the obsidian shards. He braced himself for the entire path to fall away from under his feet, taking him and the Toma to their dooms. The infected beasts, momentarily dazed, looked at him with malice in their eyes. Once again their swords rose up to strike him. He tried to take a step back to get out of their reach, but his foot slid on the fluctuating glass and he painfully crashed to one knee. In an instant he felt the hot piercing pain of obsidian shards cutting through his pants and into his skin. He cried out, accidentally gasping in a lungful of the mushroom spores that had begun to fill the air once more. Behind him he heard the cries of his companions. He didn't have time to look back at them before the Toma's swords slashed through the air in his direction.

Eighteen

Tyler clenched his eyes shut, bracing for the impact of the rusted blades. He knew he was dead before they struck. Even if the Toma somehow missed, which was unlikely, his lungs were already full of fungi spores. It was only a matter of time before they took over his body and forced him to become a host for their procreation, spreading the curse of the Blightwood further through the land. Instead of helping the people of Bramoria, his body would be used to make it uninhabitable and dangerous. In his last moments he wished there was some way he could say goodbye to his friends, to talk to Danny one more time, but kneeling there with razor sharp shards of glass working their way into his body, he knew it would never be.

But instead of the jagged edge of the Toma's rusted blades, Tyler heard the shrill screams of the infected beasts. His eyes flashed open as a rush of hot air washed over him once more. To his right a massive plume of bright blue flame erupted out of the ground, a haunting and ethereal cry rising up within it. The fire twisted and changed, forming itself into a massive peacock-like bird with its wings outspread and long tail feathers trailing behind it. In a flash it rushed the Toma, the fungi and remaining fur on their bodies bursting into flames in an instant. The bird swirled around them, mercifully snuffing out their lives one by one and finally putting them out of their misery. Spores and bodies burned until there was nothing left but hot embers floating on the breeze.

Tyler watched on, stunned into silence by what he was seeing. He knew it must be the Sage's phoenix, but he didn't understand how it was there. Koto told him it had died, the phoenix burning away into nothing, leaving behind only the strange crystalline stone. But as the questions raced through his mind with no answer the phoenix turned to face him. With another haunting cry it dove through the air, its flaming body heading straight to Tyler.

He barely had time to close his eyes before the fire enveloped him. In an instant he felt himself lifted off the ground, the deafening flames roaring all around him. The heat was more intense than he thought possible and every inch of his skin felt as if it was on fire. A sharp pain pulsed through his body as the obsidian shards were ripped from his leg by some strange force. He cried out at the sudden pain and felt the fire instantly invade his body, rushing down into his lungs, burning the air out of them in a flash. He wanted to scream, but nothing came out. It felt as if the fire would burn him from the inside out and he found himself wishing it would so he wouldn't have to bear the pain any longer.

Just as his vision was tunneling in and he was on the verge of blacking out, the pain began to recede. Gently his body was lowered to the ground, a newly formed sheet of solid obsidian glass under him instead of broken shards. The flames turned from blue to purple before coalescing into a golden sphere hovering over his chest. He watched as it slowly began to shift, forming a familiar shape before the color began to fade and darken. In the blink of an eye the golden light disappeared completely and all that was left behind was what looked to be a freshly hatched bird with mottled orange and red feathers.

The first thing to cross Tyler's mind was that it was kind of cute. A second later he wondered why he hadn't been burned alive by the flames. But before he could process that thought, he saw both Ninsar and Koto skid to a halt next to him, kneeling down on the sheet of glass at his side.

"Are you alright?" Koto gasped, reaching forward and grabbing Tyler by the shoulders. "What was that? What did you do?"

"Don't get too close!" Ninsar said, keeping her head away from him. "He could still be infested with spores!"

"After all that fire?!" Koto snapped back. "How about we look him over before we pronounce him a lost cause, huh?" Koto turned back to him. He lifted Tyler's head gently turning him from side to side. "Can you hear me?"

"Y-Yeah," Tyler managed to say, his throat so dry he could barely speak. He glanced at Koto's pack. "W-Water."

"Don't!" Ninsar hissed as Koto took out his water skin. "It'll just feed the spores!"

"Ninsar," Koto replied with a biting tone, his fangs bared. "I'm saying this nicely once. Back the fuck off."

She opened her mouth to retort, but snapped it closed once more. Koto helped Tyler to sit up a little and there was a small chirp from his lap as the bird was jostled. Tyler reached out and cupped it with one hand while taking the water skin with the other. He drank greedily, savoring the cool bite against his parched throat. As soon as he pulled it away he dropped it beside him and used his free hand to check himself over. Touching his face and neck he expected to feel char and burns, but there was nothing there but smooth skin. His eyebrows, hair, and even his eyelashes were intact and there didn't look to be a single scorch mark on any of his clothing. However, the spores that had dusted his clothing were gone and when he ran his fingers through his hair, they came back clean with no hint of the fungi left behind.

Another chirp caught his attention and he glanced down at the small bird cupped in his hand. It was no bigger than a softball and strangely warm to the touch, the downy feathers radiating heat from its tiny body. Tyler knew instinctively it was the phoenix, but didn't understand why or how it had come to be. Only a few moments before he'd been carrying around what he thought was a stone, but the longer he stared at the little bird, the more he began to wonder if it had actually been an egg. He held out his other hand to the small creature, letting it examine a finger for a moment before running it over the top of its head. The chick closed its eyes and purred almost like a cat, the sound strangely melodic.

"Is this what I think it is?" Tyler asked, looking back up at Koto.

"I... I don't know," he replied, staring at the bird for a long moment. "I've never seen a baby one before."

"Oh please, let's worry about the fucking bird. Sure," Ninsar scoffed. "Need I remind you both that we're still sitting on a path that could erupt into flames at any moment?!"

Tyler looked up at her, then to the small cracks and crevasses where the earth had split open around him. All, including the one the egg had fallen into, were dark and cool, almost as if nothing had ever happened. He glanced down the path in both directions, craning his neck over his shoulder. The thin trails of smoke were disappearing and the stench in the air had already begun to subside. He looked back to the little bird cuddled against his hand.

"I think the bird calmed the volcano..." he said with trepidation. "At least for now."

Ninsar looked up at Koto. "Great. Now he's fucking crazy."

Koto shook his head. "I don't think he's wrong. Look at the rest of the path."

She glanced over it for a long moment. "Fine. The tiny magic bird killed the volcano. Now can we please get off this fucking road before we're killed by something else?"

With that she stood up and walked away, heading down the Obsidian Path to the other side of the mountain. Tyler ran his finger over the bird's head, watching her go.

"What's her problem?" Tyler asked incredulously. "This little guy just saved us and she's still pissed."

Koto sighed. "She's got a lot on her mind."

"*She's* got a lot on her mind?!" Tyler scoffed. "I literally almost died a moment ago, I still might if those mushroom spores are in my body, my best friend is trying to murder me while the other slowly dies, and I'm somehow supposed to do something about all of that." He pointed to Ninsar who was now at least a hundred feet away. "What does she have to be worried about?"

"Everything you just said," Koto replied calmly but firmly. "You have control over all those things you just mentioned. She does not."

He sighed, reaching out a hand to help Tyler to his feet. "Imagine having all those problems with no power to do anything about them. You're her only hope for Tiragan to survive and it's no secret she finds you somewhat incapable."

"Wow. This is turning into the best post-almost-died pep talk I've ever had."

"I didn't say I think you're incapable," Koto retorted, giving Tyler a harsh look. "I'm just trying to help you understand what she's feeling."

"Well maybe she needs to understand what I'm going through."

Koto shook his head, pinching the bridge of his nose. "You two are impossible." He waved Tyler on, scooping up the nearly empty water skin from the ground. "Come on. Let's keep moving. The faster we get to the Sage, the faster you two stop trying to kill one another with biting remarks. That and I'm tired of being attacked every other day."

Tyler wanted to reply, to say something snarky back, but at that moment he felt a sharp peck on one of his fingers, pulling his attention back to the chick held there. "What do you want?" he asked, his tone not the nicest.

There was another peck immediately and he hissed through his teeth at the pain. He stared down at the tiny creature, its black eyes staring back at him. If he didn't know any better he'd guess the bird was telling him to keep his mouth shut. Brushing the thought away, he began to pet the top of its head once more.

"When we stop, I'll find you some worms or something," he said to the chick. "That's what birds eat, right?"

The purr that followed felt like a 'yes'.

THE REST OF THE DAY passed by in silence save for a few words here and there when it came time to find a place to camp for the night.

Koto was the first to spot a suitable place inside the forest, a small hollow inside a circle of trees. They'd left the mountain behind in the late afternoon, finally descending to its base. From there Tyler could just make out the trails of smoke slowly starting to fill the sky once more, the magma below the surface active again. His gut told him the phoenix was responsible, but his logic didn't want to agree.

As Ninsar and Koto gathered wood for their fire, Tyler stayed behind, sitting between the roots of a tree to rest from the taxing day. He placed the bird gently on the ground and took out his dagger. Using the blade to cut through the dirt and root hairs, he dug himself a small hole. Before he even got a chance to retrieve any of the multitude of bugs and worms he'd uncovered, the bird pushed his hand aside and dove in. He watched as it greedily gulped up any insect too slow to evade its beak. A small part of him was relieved the bird could gather its own food since he wasn't overly fond of bugs in the first place. Butterflies and moths were one thing, but something about the ground dwelling variety made him squirm.

In a matter of moments the chick had picked the dirt clean and sat back at the edge of the small hole, tilting its head back and forth in search of more food. Twice more Tyler cut through the soil and let the bird feast. Halfway through the third hole the chick started to grow sluggish, its movements indicating that it was losing interest in food and its belly was already bulging. Once it had stopped trying all together, Tyler scooped it up and took a seat on one of the large roots pushing up from the ground. There Koto was already in the process of starting the fire and getting their small hollow ready for the night.

"Did you feed it?" he asked, not looking up from the embers he was slowly coaxing into flame.

"Yeah," Tyler replied, stroking the top of the bird's head as it nestled against him. "Hungry little thing." He glanced down at the chick, feeling the heat rolling off its body. "Is it normal for birds to be almost hot to the touch?"

"I'm not sure about other birds, but I'd say it's probably normal for a phoenix," Koto replied. He leaned back as the kindling began to crackle, the fire finally taking hold. "I can't say I know much about phoenixes. As far as anyone knows, the only one to ever exist has been the companion of the Sage since he came to Bramoria." He eyed the bird, tilting his head back and forth. "He's probably the only one that knows anything about them."

"I mean, but we know the basics, right?" Tyler said. "Phoenixes have healing powers, they control fire, and are a symbol of life and rebirth." He glanced down at the small bird. "I've heard when they die they are reborn again from the ashes. That's when I saw the stone I didn't think anything of it. I had no idea it would be an egg."

Koto stared at him.

"What?"

"You continually impress me with your knowledge of magical things even though you're not from our world."

Tyler shrugged. "This is just normal mythology back in my world. It's nothing special."

Koto simply nodded. "Did you ever feel anything from the egg? Any movement at all?"

"No," Tyler shrugged. "It was always warm, but that was it."

Koto leaned forward, resting his chin on his hands. "It must have been the magma that woke it. The intense heat sped up the process." He reached out a clawed finger and stroked the downy puffball in Tyler's hands. "I'm sure the Sage didn't intend for him to hatch before you got back, but I'm glad he did."

"He's the only reason I'm still alive." Tyler lifted his gaze to Koto. "I... I think he got rid of the mushroom spores too."

"Oh?"

"I felt the fire inside me, deep in my lungs. I... I think he burned them out."

"That would explain why you're not showing any symptoms yet," he nodded. "The Blightwood fungus takes effect within a couple of hours. You can see the roots in the eyes and mushrooms grow from the ears and nose first." Koto reached forward and grabbed Tyler by the chin, turning his head side to side. "But you're not showing anything. You look as if you never came into contact with it at all."

Tyler felt his heartbeat quicken as Koto held his face to the growing firelight. For a moment he held Koto's gaze, but as soon as the fingers left his chin he looked away. The feeling was strange and it kept coming back. It didn't feel completely unfamiliar, but he didn't understand why it kept coming up. The only time he'd had similar reactions was around Danny, but those had subsided with time. However, these new feelings seemed stronger and more raw, something he wasn't very familiar with. He'd been so preoccupied with getting into college and avoiding the world that he'd never given such things any thought.

A small chirp drew his attention downward and he watched as the bird in his lap settled into the folds of his clothing, its little black eyes closing as it puffed itself up. Tyler smiled and ran his finger over the chick's head, flattening the ruffled orange feathers. It purred again under his touch.

"Well, it's cute, I'll give you that," Ninsar said as she dropped an armful of wood to the ground and plopped down beside the fire. She glanced over at Koto who was trying to make himself look busy. "You checked him over?" she asked, gesturing to Tyler. "He's not gonna turn into a monster and infect us in the night is he?"

Tyler felt the heat of irritation flare in his cheeks, driving away the rest of his emotions.

"He's fine," Koto replied without looking up.

"How is that possible?" Her piercing gaze turned to Tyler, looking him up and down. "I watched him inhale the spores."

"It seems that he–"

"*He* knows how to talk," Tyler spat, cutting Koto off. He continued to glare at Ninsar. "You don't need to keep talking about me like I'm some child."

"Ha!" Ninsar scoffed, her eyes narrowing. "And yet, that's exactly what you are. A big spoiled fucking baby."

Tyler was on his feet in a flash, the small bird rolling off his lap and into Koto's outstretched hands. "What the *fuck* is your problem, huh?" He pointed back to the volcano through the canopy. "I nearly died today and all you can do is sit here and be a fucking bitch to me! What the hell did I ever do to you?"

Ninsar stared up at him, the muscles in her cheeks as hard as rocks as she clenched her jaw.

"You know, for half a fucking second I thought you and I could be friends. You've helped us a lot and got us out of some bad situations. Hell, I even told D–Tiragan to go talk to you about how he felt because I thought you'd at least be decent to him." Tyler felt the heat rising in his chest. All the pain and anger he'd been feeling for weeks was rising to the surface in a flash. "All I've been doing since I got to this fucking place is trying to save my friend and nearly dying myself every other step of the journey! And yet you never give me a fucking break even though I'm doing everything I possibly fucking can to be better." He lifted a finger, pointing it viciously at Ninsar. "I take back what I said to Tiragan. He doesn't deserve you... he deserves *better* than you."

Tyler almost regretted the words the moment they came out of his mouth. He watched as Ninsar jumped to her feet, her fists balled at her sides. She looked somewhere between murdering him on the spot and bursting into tears. For a long moment they stared at one another, neither backing down from their fury. Then, without warning, both of them turned away and stormed off in opposite directions, drifting deeper into the Blightwood and out of sight of the campfire.

Nineteen

Tyler sat in the darkness with his back against a large oak tree. The roots slithered across the ground creating a small alcove where he was seated. Above him the leaves danced in the night breeze, filling the woods with their song as night drew closer. The air was filled with the smell of damp earth and life, but all of it went unnoticed. In his mind thoughts raced, most of them fueled by anger toward Ninsar and the entirety of Bramoria. For the first time since coming to that strange place he was feeling confident in his abilities and still she wouldn't give him the time of day. It seemed no matter what he did, his thoughts and actions were met with animosity. Even if he did partially regret his words to her, he didn't regret his anger.

Reaching down, Tyler ripped a handful of grass and leaves from the ground, throwing them into the surrounding trees. His hand met a large stone on the second grab and he hurled it into the darkness. A moment later he heard the stone strike a tree and the hollow wooden sound echo through the forest. Still he sat back with his arms crossed. Nothing, not even his outbursts, seemed to help him feel better. He knew he needed to get to Danny, to save him if he could, but merely the act of journeying was almost too much for him to handle. The sheer frustration he felt at the entire situation made him want to scream. Every step he took was fraught with peril and even when he overcame it, he was only met with hostility.

"Are you alright?"

Tyler spun around, nearly knocking his head against the tree in the process. He'd been so caught up in his own thoughts that he hadn't heard Koto's approach. Then again, he was nearly silent when he wanted to be.

"No," Tyler huffed, leaning back against the tree once more. "I haven't been alright since I got here."

Koto walked around the tree and took a seat on an upraised root near him, the small phoenix still cradled in his hands. Tyler glanced at the bird, noticing the tiny glare it was giving him. Even the fucking bird was mad at him.

"So what's it going to be this time?" Tyler asked, not waiting for Koto to speak. "An intervention? A talk about how I should take it easy on Ninsar because she's having a hard time too? Maybe you'd like to lecture me about being a better person."

There was a long pause as Koto stared back at him, the look in his eyes betraying his emotions. "None of those things actually." He pushed himself back to his feet. "I came back here to check on you, but if you're just going to be an asshole, I think I'll go back to the fire."

"What do I need to do to convince her I'm not an idiot?" Tyler sighed, his eyes lifting to meet Koto's. "I get it, I fucked up and got Faus killed. I already feel bad enough about that. I mean... I literally watched the guy get his heart torn out of his chest. That day is going to haunt my dreams for the rest of my life." He huffed, dropping his head back toward the ground. "I've nearly died half a dozen times and it seems like everything wants to kill me. But I've been getting better haven't I? I haven't died yet and I even fought away those Toma by myself. How much more suffering and fighting do I have to go through to make her stop treating me like shit?"

"Have you talked to her about it?"

"We've talked a couple of times, but not about that specifically." He paused. "I... I actually thought we were making some progress there for a minute. She was decent to me for the first time back in Zoethaven. I guess I thought it would last."

"Maybe this is just the way she communicates."

"Well then good riddance," Tyler scoffed, crossing his arms over his chest once more. "I'm not gonna put up with that bullshit."

A hand suddenly grasped the front of his shirt and hauled him to his feet. "You will follow me," Koto commanded. "We're going to put an end to this once and for all."

"Let me go!"

Koto leaned in with his brows furrowed and a snarl on his lips that displayed his elongated canines. "I said, follow me."

Tyler grumbled, but he did as he was told. As soon as they arrived back at the fire, Koto stuffed the phoenix into his hands and told him to wait, tromping off in the opposite direction. For a few minutes there was silence, then Tyler heard raised voices and eventually the shuffle of feet through fallen leaves. Koto reappeared at the edge of the firelight once more with Ninsar in tow. She looked about as grumpy as Tyler felt and he turned away, not even wanting to look at her anymore. Koto crossed back through and took the small bird from Tyler before leading him to the other side of the fire, stopping only a couple of feet from Ninsar.

"You two are behaving like children," he said venomously. "And I'm tired of listening to you two fight constantly, so we're going to get it over with."

Both Ninsar and Tyler looked up at Koto, not understanding his meaning. He took a step back, stroking the small bird in his hands. He reminded Tyler very much of a certain evil villain he'd seen in a series of stupid movies about a british spy. Tyler waited for some ridiculous anecdote to follow or a stern lecture. That always seemed to be Koto's method.

"Both of you will lay down your weapons at my feet." He stared at the pair of them, neither moving. "I said," he growled through clenched teeth, "put down your weapons."

For a long moment they both stared at him. Eventually Ninsar let out a sigh and pulled the sheath from her belt, dropping the sword in the leaves beside Koto. It took her a moment longer to remove the four daggers she had hidden on her person, three of which Tyler didn't know about. He watched until she finished and crossed her arms once more, staring at him expectantly.

Tyler protested. "I don't underst–"

"Put down your weapons," Koto repeated, cutting him off.

Tyler gave him one last hard look before he followed suit. He removed the sword from his left side and the dagger from his right. Tossing both of them at Koto's feet he placed his hands on his hips.

"So now what?"

"Now, since the pair of you want to act like children, that's how you're going to settle this." He gestured to the pair of them. "Fight."

"What?"

"I said fight. Hand to hand, no weapons needed. Fight until you get it out, you feel better, one of you falls, or you by some miracle become friends. I don't care how you do it, just get it over with."

"Fine by me," Ninsar smirked, rolling up her sleeves.

"I don't want to fight," Tyler replied, glancing over at Ninsar.

"You could have fooled me," Koto said coldly. "All you two seem to do is pick fights with one another."

"But..." His gaze flicked back to Koto. "I... I can't."

"And why is that?"

"Because he's a piece of shit coward," Ninsar cut in. "That's why."

"No that's not why!" Tyler yelled back. He sort of shrugged and gestured oddly in her direction. "She's... well she's a girl!"

"I don't see what that has to do with anything," Koto said, his face unwavering.

"You're not supposed to hit girls!"

"Well then, you're more than welcome to just stand there while I beat the shit out of you," Ninsar laughed. She nudged Koto in the shoulder. "Remind me to thank you for this. I'm going to enjoy it."

"On the count of three you will fight," Koto continued, ignoring Tyler's plea. "You will not stop until one of you falls or surrenders."

"You can't be serious..."

"One."

"Seriously Koto, this isn't funny."

"Two."

"I'm not going t–"

Before Koto could finish the count, Tyler felt a fist collide with the side of his jaw, lifting him off his feet and throwing him to the ground, the air rushing from his lungs as he hit the earth. Stars danced across his vision and an intense pulsing filled his face as pain radiated across his skull and neck. He gasped and coughed, trying to force breath back into his lungs. The metallic tang of blood filled his mouth as he looked at the figure standing over him. Ninsar had a wide grin pulling at her features, the firelight giving her an even more menacing look. He couldn't believe she'd actually punched him.

"What the fuck?!" he yelled in her direction. "He said on the count of three! You cheated!"

"Rules are for idiots and those too weak to break them," she chuckled. "And you're both."

He looked over at Koto. "You're not going to do anything?"

Koto didn't respond, he just stood there with the small bird clasped in his hands, watching the scene in front of him unfold.

"Are you gonna get up?" Ninsar asked, stepping into his line of sight. "Or do you give up already?"

"Fuck you," he hissed back at her.

He'd been planning to surrender immediately, but not that she'd decked him, that was off the table. Slowly he started to get back to his feet, rubbing his jaw where a bruise was already forming. However, before he'd stood all the way up he saw a quick movement out of the corner of his eye as Ninsar dropped low. In less than a second his legs were swept out from under him and he tumbled back to the dirt and leaves, landing painfully on his elbow.

"Too slow," she chided.

Tyler didn't respond. Instead he lashed out with a cry of rage, arms whizzing through the air in a vain attempt to land a strike. Ninsar's movements were lazy as she dodged, laughing at him the entire time.

"You're pathetic. You shouldn't worry about fighting girls, you'd never be able to hit one flailing around like that," she smirked, dancing out of his reach. "It's no wonder you can't do anything to help your friends. You're too busy feeling bad for yourself to bother with them or learn to actually protect them." She stared down at him, her grin shifting to a look of disgust. "You're a pathetic little boy. I don't know what the Sage sees in you." She spat in his direction, the saliva landing on his shoulder and soaking into his clothing. "The only reason he's chosen you is because you're all that's left. You're worse than the bottom of the barrel."

Tyler's face was on fire both out of embarrassment and rage. Everything she said fed into his worst fears. The little voice inside his head had been telling him how pathetic he was for a long time and how unfit he was to save anyone. He couldn't even stand up to his own mother, so how was he supposed to save Danny or stand up to Clay? A part of him wanted to lay down in the dirt and just give up, but then a new voice spoke, one filled with fury at his own feebleness. It told him to get up, to do exactly what Ninsar said and stop feeling bad for himself. Hadn't he stood and faced the Toma by himself? There was something inside him that wanted to fight, something that screamed at him to stand up for himself. For a long time he'd been trying to force it down to live up to everybody else's expectations, sacrificing his own choices to not disappoint his mom or his friends. But this time he felt it clawing towards the surface and instead of forcing it back down, he set it free.

Slowly he pushed himself to his feet. Ninsar, seeing him trying to get up again, spun around, her leg whizzing through the air toward his shoulder. Tyler's hand flashed forward, catching her by the ankle and redirecting it. The momentum threw her off balance and she nearly went down, her eyes lifting to stare at Tyler.

"Not bad," she murmured, regaining her balance easily. "There's some fight in you after all."

Instead of giving into her goading, Tyler leapt forward, driving his fist toward her face. She saw the punch coming and managed to avoid the majority of it, although his knuckles scraped the side of her chin as she dodged to the side. Her expression was one of surprise as her lips twisted into a smile. Tyler widened his stance and lifted his fists, remembering all the things Koto had taught him.

"Look who's standing up for themselves for once," Ninsar sneered. She raised her own fists, keeping her elbows tight to her body. "It's about time you started taking some of this seriously."

Tyler rushed her again, but this time she was ready. His punch went sailing through the air, easily missing her by more than a foot. The momentum nearly sent him back to the ground, but he recovered quickly, turning back to face her maniacal smile once more.

"Look at all these emotions you have bottled up," she said, gesturing to his entire body. "And yet nothing comes of it. Even when you finally explode and let it all out, you're still just a pathetic little worm." She took a step forward, dropping her arms to her sides. "Tiragan is going to die if you don't start shaping up and it'll practically be your fault!"

His fist flew through the air, his body reacting before he even knew it was happening. Ninsar lifted a hand and caught it, stopping the punch dead in its tracks. The sound of his fist striking her palm echoed through the trees.

"Shape up?!" he cried. "You don't think I can do anything anyway, so what's the fucking difference?"

"Here's a lesson for you," she said, leaning close. "It doesn't matter what *anybody* thinks of you or your choices, what matters is what you *can and will* do." Her hand grasped around his fist, twisting his arm painfully to the side. "I can read you like the pages in a book, Tyler. You'd rather stand by and watch others live than do it yourself. You're nothing but a sad little boy who's too afraid to make his own decisions."

"I am not!" he yelled, ripping his hand free.

"Then prove it!"

Tyler felt the anger coursing through his body as he threw punch after punch, all of them easily deflected by Ninsar. With each failed attempt her smile grew until it had turned into a malicious laughter. The sound of it drove him wild with fury. His moves became more erratic and she used his carelessness to land her own strikes against his ribs, back, and chin, filling his body with pain.

"You're not going to save anyone like that," she laughed. "Tiragan would be dead already if he was relying on you."

With a roar of rage, Tyler flung a fist in her direction. Ninsar caught it, spun him around, and socked him in the gut, the blow driving all the air from his body. He slumped down to the ground clutching at his belly, tears streaming down his face from the pain.

"I... I hate you," Tyler gasped, trying to force the air back into his lungs.

A hand wrapped around his collar and hauled him to his feet. Ninsar's face was inches from his own, her eyes filled with fury.

"You don't hate me," she snarled. "You hate yourself. That much has been clear since the moment I laid eyes on you." She cocked her head to the side. "And you want to know who's fault it is? Yours." She glanced over to Koto who was still watching silently, albeit with a worried look on his face. "Tiragan told me all about you," she continued, turning back to him. "About all your little *secrets* that you think you've been hiding. About not wanting to leave home, being too afraid to live your own life, always blaming everyone else for your problems silently while you allow them to get worse and worse." She pulled him a bit closer, her voice barely above a whisper. "He's known about your little crush you've had on him for a long time. I guess you were just too pathetic for him to feel the same way."

A resounding crack echoed through the clearing as Tyler's fist collided with the side of Ninsar's face. Her hand let go of his collar as she stumbled back and he dropped down, sweeping her legs out from under her. In a matter of seconds she was on the ground, her hair and face covered in dirt and leaves. She held a hand to her bruised jaw, staring back up at him.

"You don't get to speak for him," he hissed through gritted teeth.

"Are you going to tell him then?" she snarled back. "Finally do something for yourself for once?"

Tyler grabbed one of the swords at Koto's feet before he could react and pointed it down at Ninsar, the tip of the blade digging into her clavicle.

"No weap–"

"Shut the fuck up," Tyler growled, his eyes flicking over to Koto. He looked back to Ninsar. "I'm tired of being treated like a moron and I'm not going to put up with it anymore."

He leaned forward, the blade piercing the pale skin. A small pool of blood began to form there and Ninsar smiled.

"Well well," she grinned. "There you are at last."

She pushed the blade aside, rolling through the leaves and out of his reach. As she got to her feet he leveled the sword at her once more. His hand was steady and for the first time in his life he felt confident and free.

"Put your sword down," she said, pushing the blade away again. "I've seen what I needed to see."

Tyler flicked the sword back to its original place. "I'm not going to let him die."

She paused for a moment. "I believe you and I'm not going to let him die either. Not if I can help it." She gave him a long hard look. "Up until this point I wasn't sure if you had it in you to do what needed to be done. Your skills are still green, but you've got some spirit. Maybe you do have what it takes to save him after all."

"I'm going to try to save both of them," Tyler replied, his sword unwavering. "But I need all the help I can get. I know I'm not perfect and I have a lot to learn, but can I count on you to fight by my side and not against me?"

Ninsar stared into his eyes. "Yes," she finally said with a nod. "And you can also count on me to call you out when you're being a fool."

Tyler smiled. "And I'll do the same when you're being a bastard," he replied. "Deal?"

"Deal."

With a flick of his wrist, Tyler threw the sword back to the ground at Koto's feet. He stepped forward and held out a hand. Ninsar took it with a smile, both of their faces a bruised and bloody mess from the fight. Koto stood a few feet away gawking at the pair of them.

"What have I done..." he murmured to himself.

Twenty

Three days of hard hiking had passed and the bruises on Tyler's face were finally starting to heal. The three of them had broken free of the Blightwood at last and began working their way through the valleys between the Dravin Peaks and the thin forests that lay between. On either side of them the mountains rose so high the tops were lost amongst the clouds most of the time. Sheer stone cliffs dotted with trees clinging to the rocks hemmed them in, giving them only one path to take. Small rivers and pools formed in the valleys from the last vestiges of snow clinging to the mountain tops. Unlike the Blightwood, the trees between the mountains were filled with all sorts of woodland life. Around every corner they ran into more creatures that watched them pass with indifference.

In the early afternoon of the third day they stopped at the base of a hollowed out cliff, a waterfall pouring into open air more than fifty feet above them. The underside of the stone was open with ferns and moss covering every available surface. There they decided to rest before ascending the side of the mountain. In Tyler's mind it was too short a rest, but he didn't complain as the three of them pushed themselves to their tired feet once more and began to climb the steep hillsides. He'd spent too much energy winning Ninsar's trust and he wanted to prove to both of them that he was just as capable as they were.

The day was late and the sun was sinking close to the horizon when they finally reached the ridgeline of the mountain. Tyler, still heaving from the exertion of the climb, stared out over the landscape that laid itself out before him. The awe and beauty of the scene would have taken his breath away if there was anything left to take. Snow capped peaks surrounded him on all sides, fading away into the distance. Stone cliffs covered in trees and waterfalls were surrounded by mist as the heat of the day began to melt away. Far below he saw the green valley where Koto said the Sage lived.

As the mists parted he beheld what he could only describe as a crystal palace. It was surrounded by colorful gardens full of trees and flowers, the entire structure placed in the middle of a cerulean blue lake. Tall glass-like spires reached into the sky coming to sharp points, their mass held aloft by faceted buttresses that glimmered and shone. Windows covered almost every available surface and what remained was delicately carved although he couldn't make out what designs they held from such a distance. Much like the crystals he'd seen at the bandit hideout and at the top of the tower in Zoethaven, the tallest palace spire caught the last vestiges of sunlight and split it, covering the entire valley in a series of iridescent rainbows dancing over the trees and the lake. It was an incredible sight to behold and one Tyler could scarcely believe.

"There it is, at last," Koto breathed, looking down at the crystalline building. "We're almost there."

The little bird in Tyler's hands began to chirp excitedly as it looked down on the valley, driving away any doubts he might have had. Finally they'd made it. They were so close to saving Danny and if he was lucky, the Sage could send them home at last. At last he could help them bring an end to the trouble Clay had been causing in Bramoria. The story was almost over.

"That's incredible," Tyler replied, his eyes trying to watch the flashes of light as they sparkled over the lake. "Do you think we can make it there tonight?"

"We can try," Ninsar said, looking over at Koto. "If you think it's safe?"

"There's a path that leads down the mountain to the lake," he replied, pointing down the ridgeline a little way. There Tyler could just make out the beginning of a switchback road heading down the mountain. "He walks these hills himself quite often, so they are well used."

Tyler looked back at Ninsar. "Are you ready to save Tiragan?"

"And stop the king?"

He gave her a nod.

"Then let's get this over with," she said, taking the lead as she headed down the ridge toward the roadway.

Koto fell in step beside Tyler as they began to follow. "You two are getting along a lot better now," he commented. "I can barely believe it."

Tyler shrugged. "I think we just had to come to an understanding."

"You mean you had to beat the shit out of each other."

"I never would have agreed with that method before, but I can honestly say it works." He reached up and massaged the green bruise on his cheek, his eye twinging a bit from the pain. "I guess there's more than one way to talk with people."

Koto lifted an eyebrow. "I'm glad I suggested it then. I thought it would just be a way for you two to get your aggression out, I didn't expect you to become buddies because of it."

"Neither did I," Tyler shrugged. He glanced up at Ninsar, her boots kicking up rocks as she picked up her pace. "As much as I hate to admit it, she was right. I have to start standing up for myself." His gaze flicked toward Koto. "It sounds stupid now, but I think a part of me has been waiting all this time for people to realize I'm unhappy. I've been sitting around hoping they'd somehow finally figure out how to read my mind so I wouldn't have to say it out loud." He ran a finger over the small bird's head. "Pretty dumb, huh?"

"Not dumb," Koto replied, placing a hand on his shoulder. "But definitely not helpful. I can honestly say I was guilty of the same thing when it came to my family. I hoped one day they'd realize who I was by themselves. Unfortunately it wasn't until after my father was dead that I learned I'd have to tell people who I was myself and what kind of person I wanted to be." He pulled his hand away, tucking it into his pocket. His arm had healed much in the past week and he seemed to be regaining most of its use. "It's a hard lesson to learn, especially when you're afraid of what being honest will do to people when you've been lying to keep them happy."

"Yeah... I know my mom isn't gonna like what I have to tell her."

"She seems to have high hopes for you."

"She does, but I'll have to live life on my own terms just like she did hers." He glanced toward the horizon where the last bits of sun had disappeared. "If I ever get back that is."

Koto stared at him for a long moment as they walked. Tyler kicked at the dirt and stones on the path, sending them rolling through the tufts of grass and down the mountain into the forest below. He felt foolish for how he'd been living, but was glad to hear he wasn't alone. There was still so much more to figure out though and going home still seemed like a far off dream. Even if he could get back, he might lose Danny and Clay along the way. He wondered what his life would be like without them, how his world would change without their influence.

Tyler felt a hand on his own, pulling him from his thoughts.

"I want to show you something," Koto said, tugging him over to the edge of the now dark path. He pointed to a small white flower bud. "Watch."

As the darkness around them thickened and the stars began to fill the sky, Tyler watched the small flower. For a minute or two it didn't move, but as the last of the golds faded from the sky he saw it suddenly twitch and begin to unfurl. The long slender petals untwisted and peeled back to reveal a glowing golden center. As it opened further the light grew, filling the darkness and casting a golden glow on the path. It was a stunning display and he inhaled deeply as the sweet scent of nectar filled the air around them. Off to his left he saw another glow out of the corner of his eye. Turning to look down the road he saw hundreds of the same flowers, all of them opening to greet the night, their petals bathing the path in golden light.

"The Sage plants these himself. They help to guide his way during his night walks," Koto explained, answering Tyler's questions before they formed. "They were my favorite part of this place for what little time I spent here."

"They're beautiful," Tyler breathed. He noticed further down the road Ninsar had come to a stop, crouching down to examine the flowers herself. "This seems like such an incredible place. I can't understand why Clay would have ever wanted to leave here."

"Hopefully the Sage can help explain that," Koto nodded, his fingers tightening around Tyler's.

It wasn't until that moment that he realized Koto still had a hold of his hand and what that could mean. Immediately Tyler felt his face flush, the heat pulsing under the collar of his shirt. A part of him wanted to squeeze Koto's hand back while the other wanted to tear it away and run. In an instant his mind became a battlefield of emotions, each side fighting one another to the death. An immeasurable amount of time passed by or maybe less than a second before he finally reacted. Gently he pulled his hand away, tucking it under his other arm with the baby phoenix.

"Koto... I... I don't think..." His heart was pounding in his chest as he searched for the words. "I can't... this isn't something I can do." He saw Koto's ears droop slightly out of the corner of his eye.

"My apologies," Koto said, his voice attempting to cover the disappointment Tyler knew he felt. "I didn't mean to make you uncomfortable."

"You didn't," Tyler replied quickly. "It's not you, I promise... it's just..."

"Just what?"

Tyler sighed, knowing he'd have to say it out loud. "I guess I don't know who I am just yet or what I'm looking for. I've never *told* anyone about how I feel sometimes... towards people like you."

Koto's eyebrows lifted. "Oh. I see." He glanced back at his feet. "Is that strange in your world?"

"Yes... and no. It depends on where you live, who your family is, things like that." Tyler was feeling worse and worse by the second as he watched Koto's reactions. "And well, I have to go home sometime, don't I? That wouldn't be fair to you. One day I'd just up and leave and what would you do then?" A thought struck Tyler suddenly. "Actually, why the hell would you even want me to begin with? I've done nothing but cause you trouble and pain since the moment I met you. Not to mention I've taken every chance I could find to prove how much of a coward I am. That doesn't sound like someone I'd see you taking interest in."

Koto lifted his green eyes to meet Tyler's, the glow of the flowers reflecting back at him. "Maybe I see something that you don't, a spark of potential and a drive to always do what you think is right even if others don't agree. I've watched you fight to find your friends with everything you have and then continue to sacrifice whatever it takes over and over to save them. I think that's pretty admirable."

"Yeah," Tyler sighed, kicking at the dirt. "And look where it's got me."

"Yes, look," Koto replied, pointing down the mountain to the Sage's palace. "It brought you all the way here, across all of Bramoria. Are you going to stand on the threshold of everything you've fought for and call it nothing?"

Tyler was silent.

"Give yourself a little credit. A month ago you were a scrawny nobody in a strange land and now look at what you've accomplished." Koto took a step closer so that he was only a few inches from Tyler. "You might not get everything you hoped for, but you did everything you could to get it." He reached up and held Tyler's chin between his thumb and forefinger. "You are more now than you have ever been and tomorrow you'll be even more. If we just put in the effort, each step taken will lead us to a better version of ourselves. Whether we succeed or fail is irrelevant."

Koto had leaned closer, the heat of his breath radiating over Tyler's lips. He wanted to lean forward, to take the kiss that was so obviously being offered to him. He'd be lying to himself if he said he hadn't been thinking about it. The past week had been filled with moments where he found himself longing for Koto to get closer, to make the first move. Now, he finally had and Tyler found himself hesitating. For a long moment he stared into those sea green eyes wondering what he should do.

It was Tyler that finally pulled away, putting some distance between them once more. "I'll try to be better about that," he said, trying to ignore the pounding in his chest. "I'm still learning not to be so hard on myself."

Koto nodded, taking a step back himself. He reached one arm across to grab the other, the gesture making him look more shy and awkward than Tyler had ever seen him.

"That's all I can ask," he said. "If you only take one thing home with you from Bramoria, I hope it's a sense of self-worth and confidence. You've earned it."

Twenty-One

At the edge of the cerulean lake there was a small dock with moss and vines growing over it. On the second to last support was tied a hempen rope, which held a small boat against the dock's edge. Tyler stared at it with bleary eyes. It had taken them nearly two hours to reach the bottom of the mountain along the flower-lit path and one more to reach the edge of the lake. Overhead the stars had gone out one by one as clouds rolled in from the west. Already he could see the faintest flashes in the distance of the thunderstorm that was on its way. All he wanted to do was get to the palace before the rain set in. A warm bed for the night would be a blessing after nearly a week trekking through the woods and mountains with little more than a bedroll to give him comfort.

Making his way to the end of the dock, he noticed the bottom of the boat held an inch or two of water. It didn't appear to be actively leaking, but unused for some time. The seats were slick with the beginnings of moss growth and here and there a small glossy blue mushroom grew from the wood. Tyler looked at the fungi with distrust. After his run in with the Toma of the Blightwood, he didn't know if he'd ever look at a mushroom the same way again. However, as there was no other means to cross the lake, each of them clambered in and untied it from the dock. Finding the oars tucked against the gunwale, Koto handed one to Tyler and together they began to paddle their way across the lake, the first droplets of rain falling down from the black sky above.

If not for the lighted windows of the Sage's palace, they would have been lost in the darkness that was nearly complete thanks to the storm. Flashes of approaching lightning illuminated their way for brief moments, the crystalline building exploding into existence as the light shone through the stone. Soon the lightning was followed by low rumbles as the head of the storm grew closer and closer. With every successive thunderclap the rain fell harder, soaking into their hair and running down the backs of their necks. By the time they were halfway across the lake, their clothing was already soaked through. Tyler shivered as he and Koto paddled harder, wanting to get out of the rain as soon as possible. It wasn't lost on any of them how dangerous it was to be the only object in the middle of a lake as the lightning drew closer.

As they approached the opposite shore, the palace loomed up from the darkness. It was much bigger than Tyler had initially thought, but he didn't have time to dwell on it. The rain was pouring in sheets now, the bottom of the boat filling further with water. In the distance he could just make out the dock and the massive crystal doors of the palace across a long yard. He wondered if Danny and the Sage knew they were coming. They'd probably throw the doors wide and invite them into safety and warmth, Danny somehow miraculously recovered and beaming once again.

It was a nice fantasy, but it was driven from Tyler's mind the moment the boat touched the dock. From out of the sky a massive bolt of lightning streaked in their direction, looking as if it would hit their small boat, killing them all in an instant. But at the last second the bolt arced to the side, striking one of the crystal spires of the palace. In a brilliant display the three of them watched the electricity race through the crystal, the entire building turning into a shimmering ball of blinding white light. All of them threw their arms up, shielding their eyes from the sudden brilliance. In his periphery, Tyler watched the entire valley suddenly explode into a rainbow of color, the facets of the stone splitting the light in all directions. It was incredible, overwhelming, and terrifying. Thankfully it lasted less than a second.

Tyler sat with a hand clutched to his chest, his heart pounding so hard in his throat he thought he'd vomit. His rain soaked clothing pressed down of him with the weight of the water and the small chick pushed itself deeper into his cloak, trying to keep away from the water. Even so its downy feathers were damp and it looked like it was shivering.

"Get me off this fucking boat before we get struck by lightning," Ninsar hissed, reaching out and grabbing hold of the dock. She clambered out and secured the rope, pulling it tight. "Come on," she said, holding out a hand to Tyler. "Let's go see Tiragan."

Despite the cold, the wet, and the constant fear from the storm, he smiled and took her hand, careful to keep the chick supported under his cloak. Ninsar helped Koto out as well and the three of them marched toward the crystal structure at a fast pace, all of them ready to finally be out of the storm.

Joy brimmed inside Tyler as they drew closer, hoping beyond hope that Danny would be standing behind the doors when they were thrown open, a smile back on his face. However, as the three of them stepped up to the door, nothing happened. After a moment, Koto reached out and wrapped his knuckles on the stone. The hollow bell-like ringing of his knock died away quickly, drowned out by the thunder and rain, but still there was no answer. Grumbling under her breath, Ninsar stepped in front and put all her weight against the door, trying to push it open. When it didn't budge the other two joined her. Digging their boots into the mud and gravel, they pushed with all their might, but still the door didn't move.

"Aaagh!" Ninsar screamed, smashing her fists against the door. "Let us in you fucking wizard bastard!"

As if on command the door shifted, swinging open just enough to let the three of them pass through, the golden light spilling out onto the grass. Ninsar stared at the door for a moment.

"Thank you," she huffed, glancing back at the other two. "I guess we can go in."

Both Tyler and Koto nodded, following behind Ninsar as she slipped through the open gap. As soon as they were within the foyer the door quickly slammed behind them, the boom echoing through the massive interior. Tyler glanced at it for a moment before turning his head toward the ceiling. Far above them were vaulted ceilings made of the same crystalline stone, illuminated by what seemed like a thousand flickering lamps. Between the vaults were detailed paintings depicting many things that he didn't understand. A few familiar shapes poked out here and there, a dragon, a wizard, a phoenix, and a series of what looked to be heroes through the ages. One, who looked very similar to Tiragan, held a sword aloft in his right hand, a bejeweled book in his left. He thought it a coincidence that the figure also had a book and wondered if he could be from a different world as well. But as he continued to stare at the paintings he noticed every single hero, no matter their weapon, gender, or race, held a book of some sort with a highly decorated cover. Each book was a slightly different color with a unique gemstone set into its center.

Tyler opened his mouth to point it out to Koto when a voice rang through the hallway.

"Ah, at last! I'd feared you'd gotten lost or ran into trouble along the way!"

Their attention was drawn to the top of a massive staircase of carved marble, a blood red carpet running down the center of it. On either side a set of spiraling banisters carved with vines and creatures led their eyes up to the man standing on the landing. He was dressed in simple robes of red and gold, although the pattern that was woven into them looked intricate. The man was older, looking to be somewhere in his late fifties, although he stood straight and tall. Under the robes he seemed thin, the assumption supported by his hard cut jaw and bony cheeks. At his side he held a gnarled wooden staff with a dark blue gem set at its apex. Tyler squinted as a shimmer of gold caught his attention on the Sage's chest. It was a golden pin wrought into the shape of a fiery phoenix.

The realization hit Tyler so hard he nearly fell over.

"Y-You!" he cried out, pointing up at the old wizard. "You're the owner of that fucking bookstore!"

The Sage smiled. "It's about time you figured it out, Tyler Wilson," he said. "Nobody steps into *The Lone Phoenix* by accident or into Bramoria for that matter." He looked over the group, as if searching for something. "Speaking of phoenixes, did you bring the egg back with you?"

"No," Tyler replied after a moment. He reached into his coat and pulled out the still damp chick. "The egg disappeared when he hatched, but I've still got him."

"Oh dear," the Sage said, his face falling as he lifted a hand to his mouth. "This is going to complicate things a bit."

"What does that mean?"

"Where's Tiragan?" Ninsar cut in, growing impatient with the pair of them. "You disappeared with him and asked us to find you. Well here we are. Now where is he?"

"Your friend... is here," he said carefully. He stared at their confused faces and sighed. "Come on, I'll show you to him."

DANNY LOOKED WORSE than Tyler had ever seen him. Every inch of his skin was covered in red splotches, giving him an almost sunburnt appearance and yet he was cold to the touch. The bed was small and stark white, similar to the hospital bed that Tyler had seen him in so many times. On his chest was placed the glowing red mage stone, rising and falling slowly with his breath. Even the stone itself seemed less vibrant than before, as if it would cease to exist without its master.

"What happened to him?" Tyler asked, the tears already forming in his eyes. "Why haven't you cured him?"

The Sage sighed, shaking his head. "I'm afraid you've placed too much faith in me. He hasn't awakened since I took him away. The most I've been able to do is stabilize him and make him comfortable." He glanced over at Tyler. "There are many things in this world I can influence, but recently I've found my abilities waning."

"You have all those magic books, the power to bring people to different worlds, and fight dragons, but you can't save him?"

The wizard stroked the small bird now cupped in his hands. "I'd planned to use the phoenix's rebirth as a last resort to help him. Death and rebirth are when they're most powerful." He glanced down at the small bird with a sad smile. "I didn't have time to wait for the egg to form if I was going to save your friend. However, I didn't think you'd need the phoenix's power again so soon. It seems he felt the need to save you along the way. If he were to force another death now to save your friend, he'd never come back and we'll need him if we're to stop the king."

"We were attacked by Toma in the Blightwood," Koto began. "They were infected and the phoenix had to sa–"

"I don't give a fuck about any of that! You need to save Danny!" Tyler cried, surging forward and grabbing the Sage by his robes. "I didn't travel all this way and nearly die a dozen times for you to tell me that it's beyond your capabilities!" He pulled the man closer, shouting into his face. "I did everything you told me to! I fought my way here, lost friends along the way, even my mother got fucking kidnapped!" Tyler pulled back, tears forming in his eyes. "I did all that and you're just going to sit here and tell me that you can't help? After all this fucking time? Why didn't you say something before?!"

"Tyler," Koto said, placing a hand on his shoulder.

"No!" he yelled back, ripping himself away. "I want to know why! Why did you let us take that book from your stupid shop? Why did you send all of us here to be tortured by this place? Why would you do that to a bunch of stupid kids?! What did we do to deserve that?"

The Sage looked down on him with an apologetic look in his eyes. "I was just trying to help, like I've done for so many others. But this time... mistakes were made–"

"Mistakes?! MISTAKES?!" Tyler screamed. "Fuck you and your mistakes! You need to fix all this before we all fucking wind up dead because of your goddamn mistakes!"

Ninsar stepped up and pointed to Tyler. "What he said."

For a long moment the Sage stood there, staring at the pair of them. Koto looked as if he wanted to cut in, but was too scared to do so. Tyler could feel his hands shaking, the tears running down his face. From the moment he stepped foot in Bramoria, everyone had been telling him that the Sage was powerful enough to save them and he'd placed all his faith in that solution. At first he'd thought Danny was lost either way, but after everything he'd learned, he knew the Sage would be able to save him. Hell, if Clay could figure it out, why couldn't the most powerful person in this make-believe world do it too?

"I've been fighting my way here for weeks because of the things you said to me. I did everything you asked," Tyler continued, his fury starting to ebb into defeat. "You gave me hope..." He sunk down to his knees, his knuckles white as his fingers pulled at the red and gold robes. "Why did you do that... if there was no way to save him..."

The Sage sighed again, a look of pity in his eyes. "There may still be hope, but it won't be easy."

Tyler looked up.

"Many things have changed since the three of you came to Bramoria and I'm afraid I'm not the wizard I once was thanks to your friend." He gestured for Koto to come over and take Tyler. "Come with me to my laboratory," he said, finally extricating himself from Tyler's grasp. "There is much that we need to speak of and decisions that need to be made."

Twenty-Two

Tyler flopped into an overstuffed chair near a glowing fireplace, his clothing still damp from the rain. Normally he'd be thankful for the heat, but truth be told he barely noticed it. His mind was too concerned about Danny, Clay, his mom, and how the fuck they were going to get out of Bramoria now that the Sage turned out to be nearly useless. He glared at the wizard as he walked around a desk and placed the small bird inside an open gilded cage. Dipping behind his desk he grabbed a leather bound tome and headed back to the fireplace, taking a seat amongst them with the book on his lap.

Glancing over at it, Tyler noticed a honey-colored gem set into the cover and the title *The Grimoire of Kings* pressed into the leather in a loopy script.

"How did you get that?" he asked, staring at the same book that Clay kept protected at all times. "Can we use that to get home?"

"It's a powerless copy," the Sage sighed, flipping it open. "It allows me to keep track of your friend and what he's up to while he's in Bramoria. I have a copy of every book in my shop here in the manor. That way I can see what my adventurers are up to and if I need to intervene." He held the pages in his hand, letting them glide across his thumb as he flipped through the entire book. "But as you can see, all of the pages are blank. Your friend has found a way to block the magic of my own making, which shouldn't be possible, and yet he's managed it." He snapped the book shut once more, setting it on a small table at his side. "I've been blind to his movements for some time now and more recently to yours as well. Although using your friend Tiragan's mage stone was foolish and potentially deadly, your contacting me was the only reason I knew you were in trouble, so I thank you for that." He leaned forward in his chair. "Using another's mage stone shouldn't be possible, but somehow you managed it. Once this is all figured out, I'd like to look into that more."

Tyler didn't respond.

"How is it possible that the king is blocking you?" Koto said, trying to fill the silence. "Aren't you the most powerful wizard in the world?"

"Yes, I am the most powerful wizard in Bramoria, but there are ways to expand one's power even beyond the level of my own." The Sage gave Koto a once over. "It's been a long time since I've seen you, Kotolor. The last time you were here your prince killed my only apprentice and both of you fled in the night." He leaned back in his chair. "Although I appreciate the communications you gave me after that day until you left the palace. They were helpful since the academy has warded the castle."

"Not very helpful it seems. I wish I could have done more to stop it all from happening," Koto sighed.

"You did what you could–"

"Yeah, and that's great and all, but how does it help us now?" Ninsar interjected, leaning against the fireplace with her arms crossed. "Tiragan is dying and the king is growing more powerful by the day. Between the book, the academy mages, and the Divinarae, he'll have enough power to snuff out all of Bramoria if he wants to."

"I was afraid of that." The Sage leaned forward, placing his face in his hands. "It confirms all of my theories about him."

"What theories?"

"That he's found the Divinarae."

Ninsar cocked her head to the side. "What do you mean 'found it'? Everyone knows where it is."

"Yes, they do." The wizard looked up at her, his face red where he'd rubbed it with his palms. "But not everyone has the only book in the world that could awaken it to its full power once more."

There was a long stretch of silence.

"You're going to need to start at the beginning," Koto said. "I've accepted that Tyler and his friends are from a different world, but I don't really understand what's going on."

The Sage nodded. "Of course. Maybe that's something we should do in the morning. You all look exhausted."

Tyler perked up at that, snapping his head in the wizard's direction. "No," he said firmly. "You're going to tell us now."

They locked gazes for a long moment until the Sage sighed once more, leaning back in his chair and turning his face to the fire.

"Alright. But it's a long story." He tapped his staff on the ground twice and a pale blue ghost-like form appeared next to him. "Please bring up tea and refreshments," he said to the ethereal figure. "And a bottle of whiskey."

With a small nod the figure turned away, took a few steps, and disappeared. Koto and Ninsar looked surprised and a little worried, but Tyler's gaze was still fixed on the Sage. He needed to know what was going on and what this *hope* was that the old man had spoken of. Whatever it was, he needed the information so he could save Danny. Leaning back in his chair, Tyler crossed his arms as the old wizard made himself more comfortable.

"Thousands of years ago," the Sage began, "there were several wizards from the cosmos who came together to create Bramoria." Koto opened his mouth, but the wizard held up a hand. "Let me finish the story first. This might be a bit different than what you've been told." He took a deep breath. "These wizards were the creators of the pool of magic that you now call the Divinarae. Although it is now seen widely as only a powerful scrying tool, it is actually the spring of magic from which Bramoria sprang, if you'll forgive the pun. We let it seep into the earth, stretching across the world to give it enough power to create life. I was one of those wizards that poured my power into the spring to create this fantastical world of beauty and magic. Although I'm afraid I'm the only one left now. The others have all left of their own volition, tired and bored with the project we once looked at with so much passion." He signed to himself, his eyes far away as if recalling ancient memories. "We wanted so badly to be gods and once we succeeded we realized how foolish we'd been. It is no small responsibility to care for an entire world.

"Anyway, Bramoria was born from the Divinarae and the veins of crystalized divicite that grew through the earth like root. Once it was in place the world began to grow and change. We used our powers to shape the landscape, grow the forests, and bring life in the form of all kinds of fauna and races of men. It was beautiful and dangerous, each of us with our own little part to look after." He raised a hand and held it to his chest. "*My* dream was to bring others here from outside worlds, those who needed it most, and show them a different perspective on life. However, when the other wizards started to leave this world, I found a real need for heroes from other realms, not people whom I could help.

"It was war that drove the other wizards away, war between the races we had so carefully cultivated with our own magic. Humans were killing dragons, kings were fighting the Veordya nation, the tribal Lacerta were nearly decimated, and the mages stayed in the shadows collecting magic and waiting for their moment to strike. We knew we could wait no longer. With my power and that of the last few wizards, we sealed away the Divinarae to keep its power away from those who would abuse it. And what we couldn't seal away, we put guardians in place to protect." He paused for a moment, a sad look in his eyes. "It wasn't long after that before I was the only one left. Just me and the last gift I ever received from my partner." The Sage looked back at the small phoenix perched in his cage, gobbling up all the food he could find. "Since that day I've been traveling between worlds with my bookshop, bringing heroes to Bramoria who could help me keep it in check, since I couldn't do it myself, and put an end to the great wars started by foolishness.

"For centuries I've kept it up, searching out those that would be the most mutually beneficial." He gestured to the shelves on the walls that were lined with leather bound tomes. "All of them did something great for Bramoria and left a better person than when they arrived." He looked up at Tyler. "And that's how I found you and your friends. Bramoria has been peaceful this last century and I was feeling confident. This time, instead of looking for heroes, I decided to seek out those that needed a new perspective on life, a chance to escape, and maybe learn something along the way. You three were supposed to be my first attempt at goodwill and charity in almost a thousand years, fulfilling my original dreams and intentions for this world at last."

Tyler gritted his teeth at the Sage's words, wanting nothing more than to leap up from his chair and punch the old man square in the nose. All along he thought they'd stumbled into Bramoria by accident because Clay had stolen a book from a strange shop. But the Sage had done it on purpose, tricking them into Bramoria to teach them a lesson.

"But some things went wrong," the wizard continued. "There were some unforeseen circumstances after your friend took the book I laid out for him."

"And what was that?" Tyler sniped, ready to see the man taken down a notch.

"In the past I chose people who were ready for adventure, who could be groomed into being heroes. But this time I wanted to help those who didn't have the best of lives, to give them something wonderful to experience for a while and maybe change their outlook on life. It was my attempt at some kind of charity." He glanced over to the fire. "But I sorely underestimated the allure of power to those who feel powerless." The Sage turned back to the three of them. "I brought Clay to my palace to teach him about this world, about magic, and about seizing control of his own destiny. Instead I found a young man so broken and vengeful that he could barely think. Not to mention, he'd already been using the book's magic a lot more than I anticipated."

"Why does that matter?" Tyler asked.

"Each book has a price," the Sage replied. "And once you use the magic within, you can't take it back."

Tyler thought back to the day he'd tried to return the book to the shop, finding it closed with a sign in the window that read 'all sales are final'. At the time he'd thought nothing of the price tag attached to the book, thinking they were all some kind of joke.

"*Your Integrity*," Tyler said, remembering the tag. "That was the price on the book." He glanced up at the Sage, his brows furrowed. "Why would you put a price like that on one of the books if it would turn the person who used it into a monster?"

"The books set their own price, I don't get to choose." Tyler lifted an eyebrow in his direction. "I know it sounds strange, but that is how the magic works."

"Then why allow people to have them in the first place? Why would you give a powerful item to someone who could abuse it? That seems really fucking stupid honestly."

"Before I would have fought you on that," the Sage said, hanging his head. "But now I know you're right. They were never meant to be more than a portal to Bramoria and I always met the users on the other side to retrieve it immediately. The world transfer alone is not enough to trigger the books to take their fee, since it's not done by the user willingly. But should the reader begin to tap into their magic on purpose, they begin to pay the price little by little." He looked at the copy of the book on the table next to him. "I decided to give Clay some time to unwind when he arrived instead of whisking him away on some adventure. I thought it would be good for him since he'd already been through so much." He shook his head. "But I was wrong. Each spell takes another tiny piece and by the time Clay arrived at my palace, he'd already used an alarming amount of magic, having discovered the power on his own. In the centuries I've been bringing people here, Clay was the first to find and access magic without help." He leaned his elbow on the arm of the chair. "I suspect it was the emotional trauma he'd been through in your world that made it possible. That kind of turmoil attracts energy of all kinds, especially magic. I knew he'd had a bad life, but I never thought he'd be able to access the grimoire on his own. Even the most advanced mages find it nearly impossible to look into the depths of those books, beyond what's written on the page. He did it almost instantly.

"But by the time I met him, more than half of his previous principles had eroded away in exchange for magic. Of course I took the book from him immediately, intent on reversing the damage as soon as possible, but he was too far gone. In less than a week he killed my apprentice, stole the book back from me, and stole a powerful magical artifact before he left. He was cold and ruthless with his execution, something he would not have been before." The Sage looked back up at Tyler. "In fact, I'm surprised he let you and your other friend live when he found you. His connection with you two must be incredibly strong for it to have withstood the power of the grimoire for so long."

"All this is great," Ninsar cut in, pushing herself away from the mantle. "But how the hell does this help anything?"

"There are a couple of things still in our favor," he replied, gesturing for her to sit down. "The first is that his power is being actively limited thanks to his impulsiveness." He glanced over to Koto. "That artifact he stole from me, the black gauntlet, was indeed magical and increased his physical fighting power greatly. However, like all magic, it comes with a price. In this case, it means he's unwillingly put a permanent tourniquet on his magical abilities, stopping him from doing anything too detrimental to Bramoria... for now."

"Too detrimental?!" Tyler cried, pointing back toward the doors to the room. "He can summon fucking dragons out of thin air and you think he's not that powerful?"

"If he were to use magic unchecked, this world would already be gone," the Sage replied in a grave tone. "You can be sure of that. Thanks to his mastery of the grimoire and uncovering the Divinarae once more, he is one of the most powerful mages in Bramoria's history. Only myself and those who came before me could stand up to him and that won't last for long if he finds other sources."

"Then why aren't you standing up to him before it's too late?"

The Sage's expression changed to one of embarrassment. "Because myself, like every other mage in Bramoria, draws their power from the Divinarae, the spring of magic. And thanks to the combined efforts of the academy and your friend, I can no longer pull from that well. I am greatly diminished."

"You said there are things working in our favor, but I'm not hearing about any except this gauntlet," Ninsar said, cutting Tyler off before he could speak again. "What else is there?"

"The second thing is Clay's connection with his friends. That could be exploited to make him remember who he is."

"Yeah, already tried that," Tyler scoffed. "And he nearly killed me. Twice."

"There's more," the Sage continued. "I believe, given enough time, that you and your friend Tiragan could stand up to him. If you work together that is. You've both shown incredible magical talent and with my aid, I believe we could stop him."

"You mean kill him," Tyler murmured.

"Maybe, maybe not. It might be possible to return him to his previous self and then–"

"What?" Ninsar cut in, her face furious. "Just forgive him? Let him keep on ruling Bramoria as the redeemed king? I don't fucking think so." She leaned down close to the Sage, her finger in his face. "You know how many people he's killed, how many he's enslaved, and what he's *done* to them... to me. That's not something you can just forgive and forget."

Tyler thought of Faus, but said nothing.

"Let us take care of him," she hissed. "Your only job is to bring Tiragan back. You've already proved your decision making abilities are left wanting."

Tyler wasn't sure he liked what she was saying, but then again, he couldn't blame her, not after what she'd been through. "Do you mean it?" he asked. "Is there really a way to save Tiragan?"

"There might be, but it won't be easy." He leaned back in his chair. "First I'll need to know the details of his illness so that I can formulate a possible cure. It's going to take some time, but with the right information I should be able to come up with something." His gaze came to rest on Tyler's. "The second is that I'll need to put him into a magical stasis, a preservation of sorts if you will. It can only last for a few days, but it'll give us more time to figure it out."

"Why do you need to do that?" Ninsar scoffed. "Too much for you to handle?"

The Sage didn't look away from Tyler. "Because if I don't, he'll be dead by morning."

Twenty-Three

Tyler lay in a soft bed, staring up at the dark blue ceiling above him. In the flickering firelight he saw the hundreds of stars painted against the dark background. Here and there he could see familiar constellations from his own world and colorful nebulas at the edges of the room. Now that he knew the Sage had helped create Bramoria himself, he was beginning to see some similarities to his own he'd never noticed before. Even so, it brought him little comfort. Not after everything he'd learned and what he'd witnessed only a few minutes before.

After their conversation, the Sage had taken the three of them to Danny's room. Recalling as many details as he could, Tyler told the wizard about Danny's illness and what it was doing to his body. He did his best to explain previous treatments and what chemotherapy was on a basic level, not that he knew much beyond that. The information seemed to be useful to the Sage, but Tyler wasn't really sure how. The majority of Danny's treatments were told to him second hand and he was merely guessing at the majority of it. Still, if it had any chance of helping his friend, he'd try to explain whatever he could.

Eventually they came to the moment he'd been dreading. Without any choice, Tyler gave his permission to Danny on magical life support, knowing they'd need the time to figure out what to do. Without any explanation of what would happen, Tyler watched in horror as the Sage cast his spell and Danny's body slowly began to turn gray. First the tips of his fingers and the ends of his hair, before it began to spread. A strange crackling sound followed the shift in color and it wasn't until it had nearly overtaken him that Tyler reached out to touch his hand. It was ice cold and made of solid stone. The sight brought tears to his eyes once more, the thought of his friend's heart coming to a stop in front of his eyes nearly killing him on the spot. The Sage explained that he would be fine and could stay that way for some time without any further damage to his body, but the touch of cold stone against Tyler's hand made him think otherwise. He wanted to believe the Sage, but faith wasn't his strong suit, not when it came to Danny's illness. Too many times he'd heard doctors deal out hope like it was free candy, only to find out later that there was no substance behind their words.

Deciding he was too exhausted to go back to the laboratory for tea and more conversation about what they needed to do, Tyler excused himself and was led to a bedchamber by one of the ghost-like servants the Sage commanded. Alone in the quiet at last, he felt the emotions well up inside him, spilling across his cheeks in the form of tears. He didn't know what they'd have to do to save Danny, but the pressure of his friend's life truly and utterly resting on his shoulders made him feel like he was being slowly crushed to death. More than once he thought about getting up and leaving the palace, abandoning everything he'd started just to ease the strain. He knew he couldn't do it, but the idea of relieving the burden of his current situation was tempting. Rolling over on his side he hugged a pillow to himself, looking for any small piece of comfort as his mind continued to race.

The passage of time dissolved into his thoughts and five minutes or possibly an hour later a knock at the door roused Tyler from his downward spiral. He glanced over his shoulder toward the door, wondering if he really heard it or if it was his mind playing tricks on him. A second knock echoed through the chamber and he turned over, swinging his legs off the bed.

"Come in," he replied, wiping his face dry.

The door slowly swung open revealing Koto and Ninsar both standing there. They were alone except for a pale blue ethereal figure that slowly dissolved behind them. Both of them looked hesitant to disturb him, but he could see the worry on their faces.

"You can come in," Tyler repeated, waving them into the room. "It's okay. I'm fine," he lied.

Koto made his way over to the bed, taking a seat beside Tyler. "Are you sure? That was a lot to take in all at once."

Tyler looked up at Ninsar who was standing a few feet away. He didn't want to look weak in front of her. "No, I'm not sure." He could feel the tears threatening again and glanced off to the side. "I just... I thought once we got here we'd finally get some answers. Everything he told me made it sound like he could help and now... now Danny... Tiragan is petrified and the clock is ticking." He looked back to Koto. "We're no closer to saving him now than we were when we left the castle." Slumping forward he placed his face in his hands, trying to shield his emotions from the other two. "I should have left him with Clay. Maybe he would have been cured by now if I had."

"Maybe he would, maybe he wouldn't," Koto said, trying to sound sympathetic. "But we all know the king is corrupted and leaving your friend with him would have spelled disaster eventually."

"But he'd be alive..." Tyler retorted. "That's what's important."

A hand came to rest on his shoulder and he looked up.

"The Sage will find something," Ninsar said, her voice lacking the confidence that he knew she was trying to convey. "He has to. And then, whatever it is, we'll make sure it happens. We're not going to lose him."

"I hope not," he sniffled. "The doctors in our world had already given up on him, but I'm not going to do that here. I'm not sure if we'll succeed, but we're in a world full of magic. Doesn't that mean anything is possible?" He turned his head back to the ground. "At least that's what all the fantasy stories we loved told us. They always made it seem like magic was the answer to everything, that it could save anyone no matter how dire the circumstances. A god, a dragon, a wizard... anything would swoop in at the last moment and save the hero when he needed it most." He glanced up at Koto. "The Sage was supposed to be that person and now... now I'm not sure if he can do it."

"Don't lose faith yet," Koto replied. "I know what we've been told wasn't the best of news, but if there's anyone in Bramoria that can figure this out, it's the Sage. I know the odds look stacked against him, but I promise he'll find a way."

"That's a dangerous promise to make," Ninsar said, raising an eyebrow in his direction, her voice holding a tone of warning.

Koto kept his eyes locked on Tyler. "And one I intend to keep."

Ninsar shook her head. "I'm traveling with the biggest pair of fools in Bramoria." She came over and sat down on the other side of Tyler. "I know we haven't always seen eye to eye, but I hope you know that we're going to do everything we can to save Tiragan."

Tyler slowly lifted his face, staring up into her eyes. "Do you really think we can do it?"

"I do," she replied, placing a soft hand on his shoulder. "Like Koto said, if there's one person that can figure it out, it's the Sage. I don't think we'd be wrong in giving him the benefit of the doubt. He's been running this world single handedly for a thousand years with a little help from heroes."

"Yeah," Tyler scoffed. "And we all know that I'm not one of those."

"Don't sell yourself short," she continued, squeezing his shoulder. "You may be naive and foolish, but I've watched you do anything to save your friends even if you were scared and that's pretty heroic as far as I'm concerned." She paused for a moment, her eyes lifting to meet his. "And you've earned my respect. That's no small feat."

Tyler smiled in spite of himself. "You can say that again," he said, his hand automatically rubbing at the bruise on his cheek. He took a deep breath and let it out slowly, glancing between the two of them, trying to calm himself. "Sorry about all that. I guess I have a tendency to get a bit hopeless. This has been a lot for me."

"The past year has been a lot for everyone," Koto nodded.

"My life has been a lot," Ninsar added with a half smile. "Not that some of it hasn't been my fault. I do like to get myself into trouble."

"I'm pretty sure you are the trouble," Tyler joked, nudging a shoulder against hers.

Ninsar punched him in the shoulder a little harder. "And I'm pretty sure you should watch your mouth before you have to tangle with me again."

Tyler glanced between them, realizing he'd somehow miraculously managed to make friends as he stumbled his way through Bramoria. From the moment he arrived he'd been trying to get home, to avoid having an adventure at all costs. Even though things were hard, he couldn't help finding some small amount of satisfaction in their company. In little ways his journey across their strange fantasy world had brought him a lot of previously unknown happiness. There was still much to be done, but in that moment he felt a tiny spark of joy.

A knock at the door pulled their attention back to the real world. Before Tyler could respond an ethereal figure stepped through the door without opening it.

"The master requests your presence in the library," the figure said, its featureless face unmoving.

Tyler cocked his head to the side. "Do you think he found something already?"

Koto shrugged. "I told you, if anyone can help us, it's the Sage."

"Well," Ninsar said, pushing herself to her feet. "Let's go see what the old duff has to say. Maybe he can actually be useful this time."

Twenty-Four

The ethereal figure led them through a series of crystalline hallways until a pair of massive arched doors rose up in front of them. Instead of knocking, the figure merely walked into the doors, disappearing into their crystal depths. There was a flash of blue light inside the stone before they swung inward silently on their invisible hinges. Inside, a room, bigger than any Tyler had ever seen, opened up before them. The ceiling was easily fifty feet above their heads, painted in the same rich fashion as the foyer and depicting what he assumed were the countless heroes of Bramoria's past. But what really caught his attention were the books.

From floor to ceiling on every wall was nothing but rows upon rows of books of all shapes, sizes, and colors. Pathways on each level wound around the room, their ornate banisters glimmering in the light of a thousand magical torches. Gilded ladders on rails appeared every twenty feet or so along the cases so that the higher shelves could be accessed with ease. In the center of the room was a series of tables, all of them stacked high in books, papers, and quills of all sorts. Against the far wall were shelves full of herbs, feathers, writhing plants, and all manner of ingredients surrounded by glass flasks of every size imaginable.

"Tale as old as time..." Tyler whispered under his breath.

"What about tails?" Koto asked, stepping up beside him, his own curling behind him.

Tyler shook his head. "Nothing."

A voice drew their attention upward.

"Ah! There you are!"

Tyler watched as the Sage descended one of the golden ladders and worked his way down a spiral staircase all the while being followed by a series of books and ingredients floating in the air around him. It reminded him of several animated movies he'd seen before, bringing a smile to his face.

"I apologize for calling you so late, but since none of you were asleep, I figured you wouldn't mind the summons." With a wave of his staff all the books and things surrounding him placed themselves on a wide circular table. One in particular landed open in front of the Sage. "I believe I've found something that could be of some use to us."

The three stepped up to the table, looking over the assortment of books. Tyler found most of them written in English, which was surprising. However, as he looked closer he noticed there was a faint shimmer to the pages and if he moved his eyes quickly enough, he found the words reverted to strange symbols and runes. He assumed there must be some sort of spell on them that translated the pages for the viewer.

"What did you find?" he asked, pulling his gaze away from the books.

"Well, I had a few ideas." The Sage pointed to a different book that propped itself against another, opening to the back third of the pages. "Since you said your friend's blood is the problem, I found several spells to remove all the blood from a body and replace it with something else."

Tyler's jaw fell open slightly. "What... What could that possibly be used for? Why would someone create a spell like that?"

The Sage shrugged. "I didn't say they were good ideas," he replied, waving his questions away. "It was just a place to start." He pointed to another book. "Then I thought maybe we could separate him from his illness physically. Just sort of pluck it all out if you will. However, the side effects of removing several pieces of the body all at once could be..."

"Deadly?"

"To put it plainly, yes. You never know what you need until it's gone." The wizard began rifling through books and ingredients laying on the table. "I thought about turning him into a creature with different blood, transforming him into a plant, using necromancy to resurrect him once he died, and feeding him an abnormally large amount of ginger."

Tyler had more questions going through his brain than he could process. "I hope those were the bad ideas."

"That's most of them, yes." The Sage turned back to him, poking him in the chest. "But then I remembered what you said about the doctors in your world using poison to kill off the illness and it gave me an idea."

For a long moment they stared at one another.

"And that was?" Tyler finally asked.

"Well, the two most deadly toxins in Bramoria are Zaba toxin and green dragon venom."

Tyler turned to Koto, a pleading look in his eyes. "How is that supposed to help?"

Koto shrugged. "You nearly died from Zaba toxin."

"Yeah, weirdly I remember that," Tyler replied. "It was terrible."

"However," the Sage interrupted. "If you combine these two toxins with the feather of a phoenix, it just so happens that they create one of the most powerful healing potions in the world called *Aquae Vitae*." He gestured to a shelf with a single glowing blue vial on it. "A single drop would make a regular healing potion like this one look like an old witch's cure." The wizard paused, waiting for a reaction, but none came. "And there's a good chance it will save your friend," he sighed at last.

"How the hell is that going to help?" Tyler sniped, feeling the irritation clawing at his stomach. "All the dragons are dead and your phoenix doesn't have any feathers yet."

"Wrong on both counts!"

The Sage pointed across the room to a small open cage where the baby phoenix was sitting. It looked terrible. Tyler squinted, noticing the patches of bald skin, the downy fluff missing in places. It had grown quite a bit since it hatched on the mountain, but to him it looked like it was on death's door.

"Is it dying?" he asked, glancing back at the Sage. "We've only been here for a few hours and it looks like it's about to croak."

"He's molting," the wizard smiled. "Phoenixes grow very quickly and they molt their baby down before they grow in real feathers. He should have several by the time you get back with the dragon venom."

"Wait... I have to go get it? You don't just have some lying around?" He turned back to Koto. "But I thought you said all the dragons were dead? Nobody has seen a real one for over a thousand years, right?"

"That's what I've been told," Koto nodded.

"No *person* in Bramoria has seen one," the Sage corrected. "But that excludes certain wizards like myself."

"Hold on a second," Tyler said, holding his hand up as the memory of his dreams came flooding back to him. "I dreamed about dragons the day I came to Bramoria. Then again about a green dragon a few days ago, it was fighting one of Clay's smoke dragon things." He looked at the others. "Nevermind. That's dumb."

"How interesting." The Sage ducked down and grabbed Tyler by the chin, turning his face side to side. "You don't have any dragon blood in your ancestry by chance, do you? Or psychic abilities? Perhaps your great-grandmother on your father's side was a witch?"

Tyler stared at him, his cheeks pinched together by the wizard's fingers. "I don't think so," he managed to mumble.

"Well, that would have been helpful." He let Tyler go with a sigh, straightening himself back up. "There is a green dragon left, but just one. His name is Ryrris and he's one of the few remaining dragons left in Bramoria. The rest of the dragons keep to the far north, buried under mountains of rock, ice, and snow. There they live in massive underground caverns big enough for them to fly freely. They have no need for the world above." He raised a finger, levitating one of the books closer, an illustration of a dragon drawn over its pages. "However, Ryrris despises the cold and has made his home on a forest island just off the western shores of Bramoria." He leaned against his staff a bit, his eyes turning toward the ceiling. "I'm afraid I'm not on the best of terms with any of the dragons, and Ryrris in particular despises me. More than one of my heroes fought and slayed dragons that had given into greed and temptation. I'm afraid they hold it against me."

"As much as I love all this wizardish whimsy you keep doing," Ninsar said in a flat tone. "Would you mind getting to the fucking point?"

The Sage gave a small huff. "The point is that you'll need to speak with Ryrris and obtain some of his venom, then return it here to me so I can cook up that potion and save your friend."

"And just how the hell are we supposed to do that?" Ninsar asked, her eyebrows furrowed.

The wizard looked at each of them in turn, pausing for a long moment as if preparing to say something wise and wizardish. "I don't know," he shrugged. "But don't tell him you know me."

Tyler lifted a hand to his face, pinching the bridge of his nose. "You've got to be fucking kidding me." He glanced back up at the Sage, his expression growing serious. "Please tell me you've got something that's going to actually help us with this. Or at least some information."

"Oh I have several things, but let's start with the first that my phoenix reminded me of." The Sage held out his hand. "May I have your bag of boundlessness so I can retrieve your mage stone?"

Tyler pulled the pouch from his belt, holding it out the Sage. "Your phoenix reminded you of it?"

"Yes," he replied, taking the pouch. "He told me your entire adventure actually in detail, or at least what he was awake for. He's quite chatty. Haven't you noticed?"

The three gave each other sideways glances as the wizard tossed the pouch to the table. They turned their attention back as he pulled the bag open and tapped his staff on the floor, the blue gem glowing suddenly. With a quick wave and a strange word Tyler had never heard before, an amber blur came flying out of the bag. In a flash the Sage caught it and Tyler saw the mage stone clutched in his hand. From within the bag he heard the muffled cries of an angry Celindra.

"This belongs to you," he said, handing it over to Tyler. "I'll deal with this one after she's had a moment to calm down." He pulled the pouch shut, cutting off the froggy rage emanating from within. "I'll let her know it was you that set her free at last."

"Her name is Celindra," Tyler said, tucking his stone back in his pocket. "If you can give her food, she'll probably be grateful. She hasn't eaten since that Lacerta in Zoethaven."

"You fed her a Lacerta?"

"She helped us with a problematic bounty hunter," Koto cut in. "He deserved it, believe me."

The Sage held up his hands. "No judgment here." He turned back to Tyler, a smile on his face. "Now, even if you set off this very moment, you would not reach Ryrris' island for nearly a month." He walked over to one of the shelves against the wall that was stacked with scrolls. "So I will get you as close as I can in the morning." Plucking a stained and yellowed roll of parchment he walked back to the table and sat it down in front of Tyler. "And you can use that to get back. It will teleport you to the top of the palace tower. After that I'm sure you can find your way back downstairs to me with the venom."

"That's great," Ninsar said, stepping up beside Tyler. "But how are we supposed to get the venom from Ryrris?"

"I'm afraid you'll have to figure that out on your own," the Sage sighed, handing over a crystal vial. "I don't know what he wants. Most green dragons love gold, treasure, and magic. I can send you with gold to bargain with, but beyond that you'll have to figure out what he yearns for." He glanced over to Tyler. "If you need to, use your stone to make him something one of a kind."

"I don't know how to do that," Tyler replied, shaking his head. "I've teleported once by accident and nearly killed us, then I contacted you. That's all the magic I've ever done." His hand went back to his pocket, his fingers tracing over the familiar stone. "I really have no idea how to use it."

"Magic," the Sage said, leaning in close, "is really very simple. All you have to do is–"

"Want something and let yourself have it?" Tyler replied with a groan. "I'm in a fucking disney movie, I swear to god."

"Actually I was going to say all you have to do is feel it and it will become true." The wizard lifted an eyebrow in his direction, but continued on. "Magic is highly intuitive. Once you have a hold of it, it will obey your every whim. The problem is when your focus wavers during a spell, then the effects can be quite devastating depending on what drew your attention away." He reached under the table and pulled out a thin brown book with stained edges. "Take that with you. It explains the basics. After that, all you need is practice."

Tyler looked around at the other three. "I really wish you all understood movies in my world, because I have at least three references to make and nobody is going to understand them." They all stared blankly back at him. With a sigh, Tyler took the book and tucked it under his arm. "Thank you. I'll work on it."

"Good," the Sage nodded. He turned to Koto. "Now you, great protector."

Koto straightened up a bit. "I... I don't need anything."

"Incorrect," the wizard replied matter of factly.

He reached out and took Koto's arm that was still on the mend and began waving his staff over it. With a few muttered words a blue mist poured out of the crystal and wound its way around Koto's arm. It grew bright and sank into the flesh until it glowed from within. After a few seconds it faded away and Koto pulled his arm back, turning it over and flexing his fingers.

"Wow," he breathed, a smile pulling at his lips. "It feels as good as new. Thank you."

"You did most of the healing yourself, I just took care of the final bits for you." The Sage turned back to one of the shelves, grabbing the single glowing blue vial and handing it to Koto. "This is the last healing potion in my possession. Keep it safe and use it only in the most dire of circumstances." He pointed to a door on the far side of the room. "I hear you're a gifted archer. Through that door you'll find the armory of heroes past and many excellent bows crafted or found on their adventures. Please take one that is to your liking."

Koto nodded. "Thank you. This is really too much."

The Sage turned to Ninsar last, a hand on his hip. "And you, the grumpy one."

Ninsar huffed, crossing her arms over her chest. "Yeah? What of it?"

"This journey was never supposed to be yours. You've had many excellent adventures of your own and I thought you'd stay in Zoethaven once you met back up with your old crew." The Sage looked over her thoughtfully, spending a long moment staring into her eyes. "But I can see the love growing in your heart for a doomed boy who showed you kindness."

"I don't know what you *think* you know..." she started.

"More than you think I should, I assure you," he replied with a smile. "But that's not important." He pointed to Tyler with his staff. "This boy needs someone to guide him. Koto is a wonderful protector, but you aren't afraid to tell the truth, to point out his weaknesses without mercy. He'll need your guidance along the way if you're to pull this off and save the one you love."

Ninsar's cheeks were red, although Tyler couldn't tell if she was angry or embarrassed.

"Okay, so what's your point?" she asked, her teeth clenched and her lips barely moving.

"Just one moment."

The Sage turned and walked to the shelves lined with ingredients and flasks nearby. However, instead of pulling an item from them, he gave his staff a wave and stepped forward, passing through the wall entirely as if it were made of air. All three of them stifled a gasp as he disappeared. Turning to one another they could all see the same question burning on their lips, but before anyone could say anything, the Sage appeared once more with a small pouch in his hand. He brought it over to the table and pulled it wide. Tyler leaned over to see another black void similar to the pouch that held the Zaba. It seemed the Sage had his own bag of boundlessness and Tyler wondered what untold treasures it could hold.

"Your eyes betray you," the Sage said with a chuckle. "After thousands of years and hundreds of heroes, I don't have much left in the way of wondrous treasures. They've been used up, lost, or destroyed across the centuries." He looked down at the bag with a sigh. "Now only a few remain." He leaned forward and reached into the bag twice, producing a silver circlet and a small stone statue of a dragon. "These are gifts for you, my dear," he said, gesturing to the items on the table as he drew the pouch closed once more. "The circlet has a simple, but powerful spell on it. Anyone who wears it has every facet of their mind sharpened. You'll find it easier to make the right decisions, see through deception, and understand those around you."

Ninsar reached down and picked up the circlet, turning it in her hands as it caught the light. "Thank you." She nodded toward the figurine. "And what's that?"

"This," the Sage said, lifting it up to her. "Is a last ditch effort to save yourselves should you find no other way out." He locked his eyes with hers. "Do *not* use it unless you have no other choice."

"What does it do?"

"It will unleash a great fury into the world once more. Long ago I managed to capture it with several of my cohorts before it got out of hand. If he's released again, he'll have to be dealt with in time before he upsets the entire world. I ask that you do everything within your power to bring it back to me, *untouched*."

Ninsar hesitated. "Why give it to me if it could do so much damage?"

"Because sometimes defeating your current enemy is required in order to make it to tomorrow. You can always live to fight another day."

Ninsar nodded, taking it gently in her hands. "I'll do my best not to use it."

"Thank you." The Sage suddenly clapped his hands together, startling all of them. "Now, off to bed with all of you! I've kept you up far too late and you'll need rest if you're to leave tomorrow." He glanced at Tyler. "And don't forget, the clock is ticking."

Twenty-Five

Tyler was awake at dawn. Despite the long night planning with the Sage, he found himself unable to sleep any longer. He'd laid awake nearly all night, staring up into the starry ceiling, thinking about what lay ahead. In his belly burned a new fire. Even with the Sage's warning that the dragon Ryrris would be hard to bargain with, Tyler felt a renewed sense of hope, purpose, and confidence. During the night of wandering and ceaseless thoughts, something had changed. Where there was once doubt, he now found conviction. Failing to save Danny was not an option any longer, no matter what the circumstances. For the first time in four years there was a *real* cure for his illness, one that would give back all his stolen life and bring some fairness back to the world. It was everything Tyler had ever wanted for his friend before they'd come to Bramoria and he'd do anything to make sure it happened. Then, once he was restored, they would put a stop to Clay's evil together. Only then could they finally go on all the grand adventures they'd dreamed about as kids and maybe find a way home when they were satisfied.

Both Ninsar and Koto had retired to their own chambers the night before and Tyler was able to dress and prepare without disturbing them. At the foot of his bed he found a chest with fresh clothing and boots exactly his size. It seemed the ethereal servants inside the Sage's palace could do most anything. In a single night they'd crafted a whole new wardrobe for him. He assumed there was quite a bit of magic involved, but he was thankful for something soft and clean to wear at last. Pulling on his boots he pushed himself up from the bed and headed toward the door. At the last moment he recalled the night with the Fossars and doubled back to grab his dagger, slipping it onto his belt before he stepped out into the hallway. Even though they were in the palace of the Sage, it was better to be prepared.

Glancing down the hallways, Tyler tried to recall which direction to go to find Danny. He wanted to visit his best friend before they set out on the next leg of their journey. It felt stupid because Danny was nothing more than a statue, but he had to see him and at least say goodbye to him. There was no option in Tyler's mind to fail, but still he wanted to remember what he was fighting for, to make the image solid in his mind. They were going to face terrible dangers and even though seeing Danny in that state hurt him, he wanted to make sure he memorized it so that it would never have to happen again.

The floor in front of him began to glow a faint blue, pulling his attention downard. Rising up like a ghost, a transparent figure materialized in front of him, giving a slight bow as he fully formed.

"Command me as you please," the figure said, the voice eerily similar to the Sage's.

"Um... I'd like to see Danny... I mean Tiragan." He felt awkward talking to a magical ghost. "Please."

"As you wish," the figure replied.

Without a sound it turned and headed down the left side of the hallway. Not stopping to think about it too hard, Tyler followed close behind, jogging to catch up at first. He was led through several winding hallways and through at least two open doorways. The entirety of the palace was silent, including the room behind the massive library doors they passed by along their route. It seemed even the Sage slept sometimes. Finally they came to stop in front of a small opaque door that Tyler recognized from the night before.

"You'll find Tiragan inside," the figure said with another bow.

"Thank you," Tyler replied. As soon as his words ended there was a small pop and the figure disappeared, leaving no traces of himself behind. "That's going to take some getting used to," Tyler whispered to himself.

He turned to face the door and took a deep breath, staring at the intricate facets cut into the crystal. Thoughts flooded through his mind and he felt a nervousness seep into his chest. It was an unexpected feeling. He knew Danny wouldn't be able to respond, but still he felt the immense pressure on his shoulders. Their mission to retrieve the venom had to work or else Danny would stay trapped in stone forever. Not to mention, there were some things Tyler wanted to say to his friend that he'd never said before.

Clearing his throat he lay a hand on the door and pushed his way in. On the other side he saw Danny lying in a bed, his skin hard and gray. Silently, he closed the door behind him, afraid any excess noise would disturb the early morning peace of the palace. With a small sigh he headed over to the bed, taking a seat on the corner. He could feel the stiffness of the white sheets under him as he sat, the fabric nearly untouched since it had been laid over Danny's form. For a long time Tyler just sat there, staring at the crystalline walls and the reflections of light within them, trying to find the right words to say.

"Hey Tiragan," Tyler said at last, staring down at his lap as he fidgeted nervously. "I'm getting better at that, you know? Remembering your name." He paused. "I wish I had been better about it to begin with. I should have asked if it was important to you, but I was just..." Tyler shook his head. "No. No more excuses. I wasn't listening and I should have been. I'm sorry."

A long moment of silence stretched out between them. There was no shuffling of servants, guests, or guards in the Sage's palace and it made everything strangely silent. Tyler could hear a high pitched ringing, although he wasn't sure if it was his own ears or maybe the palace walls themselves.

"Well, we're leaving today," he finally said. "We've got a bit of a fetch quest to do, one of those things that's right up your alley. Apparently the Sage thinks if we go steal some venom from a dragon, it can cure you. It sounds like the kind of stupid shit you'd read about in books or have to do in a video game." Tyler laughed to himself, feeling the tears well up unexpectedly. "I wish you could go with us," he murmured, his voice cracking. "These are the kind of adventures you've always longed for and now that we're finally having them... you're stuck here." Tyler reached up and used his sleeve to wipe his cheeks. "But

I want you to know that I'm not going to fail, okay? I'll make sure we get what you need and once this is all over and you're back on the mend, we'll go out into Bramoria and have the adventures you've always wanted. We can go wherever the wind takes us and beyond. At least for a little while."

Tyler glanced at his friend's face frozen in stone. He looked so peaceful, almost like he was sleeping. If it had been a statue, some might have called it angelic, but even the thought of saying that made him feel stupid.

"I'm sorry I didn't help you sooner," Tyler sighed, leaning his face into his palms. "I know it's just an excuse, but I was just so afraid of everything. Afraid of you dying, afraid of telling my mom I didn't want to go to college... afraid of telling people how I felt." He glanced over to Tiragan. "But I'm not going to be afraid anymore. You know me better than anyone, so this won't come as a shock to you, but I don't want to go to that college or any for that matter. Mom wanted that for me and I just don't. I'm gonna tell her too, just as soon as she's free of Clay's spell. And I'm going to start standing up for myself." A smirk spread across his face. "Believe it or not, Ninsar and I got into a fist fight. And what's even stranger is that I learned a lot because of it. She's been right all along of course and it took getting my ass kicked to realize I was doing everything she'd accused me of." Tyler shook his head. "I don't know what you see in that woman romantically, but I definitely respect her."

He glanced back to Tiragan once more, the nervousness creeping into his chest again. Taking a deep breath he forced it back down.

"She told me, you know," he sighed. "That you've known how I felt about you for quite a while. I'm not sure I really believed myself when it came to that, but the more I start to face myself, the more I realize it's the truth." He leaned over Tiragan, staring down at him. "I've loved you for a long time... and I think you love me too, but just not in that way." He paused for a moment, a smile coming to his face. "I hope you know I'm not mad about it, but I wanted to tell you at least once." Tyler leaned back with a groan. "Oh great, that's another thing I'm going to have to tell my mom. She's gonna love that. You know she's been planning on me getting wifed up and having like a dozen kids? First of all, who the hell wants that many children? And secondly... I don't have to live up to her expectations anymore. Hopefully she understands that's not the kind of life I'm going to lead and is okay with it. We never really talk about that kind of stuff and I'm scared to tell her, but like Ninsar said, it's time I stand up for myself." He slapped his hands on his knees and pushed himself to his feet. "And that's what I'm going to do. Once we get you back on the mend we'll go face Clay together. Who knows? If I can save you, maybe together we can save him too... although I'm not sure if he deserves it anymore."

Walking over to the head of Tiragan's bed, Tyler placed a hand on the stone forehead.

"But we'll deal with that once I get back. For now, I've got a dragon to go make a deal with, so wish me luck." He paused for a moment before leaning down and placing a small kiss on his friend's stone cheek. "I promise I'll save you. Just don't give up on me."

For a long moment Tyler stood there in silence, watching over his friend and wondering if he could hear anything that had been said in the past few minutes. It seemed almost cliche, like those people who talked to coma patients in movies, but still it seemed to raise his own spirits at the very least. The weight had somewhat lifted from his chest and for the first time in years he felt like he could breathe.

"Alright Tiragan, it's time for me to go on that adventure. Wish me luck." Tyler walked back to the door, taking one last glance over his shoulder. "I'll be back soon to take you on your own. I promise."

A COUPLE HOURS AFTER dawn the trio found themselves at the top of the Sage's tower. All of them wore new clothing, freshly cleaned leather armor, and were sporting finely crafted weapons. Koto's armor was a forest green and the bow over his shoulder looked like it had grown naturally from the crook of a tree, the fine bark preserved under a sheen of polish. A fine silvery thread connected either end while at least a dozen black fletched arrows filled a quiver on his back. Ninsar, on the other hand, wore armor stained almost black, her blonde hair in harsh contrast to her dark accouterments. At her side was a golden-handled rapier with a ruby set into the pommel. Tyler's armor was a normal brown that matched well with his plain traveling clothes. Over his shoulder was a plain leather bag matching those of his companions, the Sage's book of magic stowed safely away within it. However, the armor did have one new feature. At the center of his chest the mage stone was mounted, the amber gem sparkling in the sun. It reminded him of Clay's armor, but instead of sharp metal edges, the leather had been crafted with the image of the sun, the rays emanating from the stone itself. Tyler loved it and the warmth of the stone against his chest was a constant comfort.

"Alright everyone?" the Sage asked, looking between the three of them. "All your things packed? Weapons, books, potions, gold, and paraphernalia?"

"Yes," Ninsar sighed, rolling her eyes. "We've been over this several times."

"It never hurts to be thorough," the wizard replied, holding up a finger. "The last thing you'd want was to be on the other side of the world without something important and only a one-way ticket back."

Ninsar opened her mouth to retort, but Tyler cut her off. "Thank you for being thorough and thank you for all your help. We couldn't do this without you."

"Don't thank me yet, there is still much danger ahead of you." He was about to turn away but stopped, looking back at Tyler. "By the way,

I let the Zaba go this morning and I told her it was your doing that brought about her freedom." He reached into his robes and produced a flask filled with a milky white liquid. "She gave me the toxin willingly."

Tyler smiled, hope swelling in his chest. "Then we have two pieces already, the toxin and the phoenix feather." He turned to his companions. "We've come this far, now let's finish it."

"We will," Koto replied, placing a hand on his shoulder. "And we'll be back with plenty of time to spare."

Ninsar placed a hand on his other shoulder. "Piece of cake."

"Well, let's not waste that confidence," the Sage said, taking a few steps backward.

Upon the floor was a large circle covered in a series of geometric patterns and runes. As the Sage stepped into the very center of it he struck his staff to the ground. With a shower of sparks the blue stone began to glow and the circle around them filled with golden light.

"On the count of three, breathe out, bend your knees, and prepare to land."

Tyler looked at Koto and Ninsar, giving them both a nod.

"One."

All three of them took a last breath.

"Two."

They forced their lungs empty, preparing for the magic.

"Three!"

With a vicious yank at the small of his back, Tyler watched as the room around him blurred suddenly as they were sucked backward into a void. The pure darkness lasted only for a moment before their feet struck something hard. Opening his eyes once more Tyler steadied himself and lifted a hand to shield his eyes from the sun. As the world came into focus he saw the three of them standing in scraggly grass at the top of a great cliff. The wind whipped up the rock face carrying the salty scent of the sea not far off. Even over the wind he could hear the crash of the waves far below as they thundered against the cliffs, the vibrations carrying through the stone.

Taking a deep breath to fill his lungs once more, Tyler caught something else on the wind besides the salt of the sea. It was smoke, almost like a campfire. Glancing down the cliff he noticed a large city placed at the edge of a half-moon shaped bay. Docks reached out into the calm cerulean waters and he could just make out the wrapped up canvas of sails on the ships docked there. However, what caught his attention the most was the trail of gray smoke rising into the air from the far side of the town and a streak of black smeared across the landscape. It looked as if nearly half the city had been burnt to the ground the night before. For a moment he wondered what had happened, but as his eyes picked up three long straight lines of burnt roofs, the rest untouched on either side, he knew what had caused it. The town had been attacked by a dragon and he was willing to bet it was one of Clay's.

Also by Blake R. Wolfe

Bone, Stone, and Wood
Exordium
Arbitrium
Profundum
The Crystal Moon

Tales of the Tellurian Pack
Alpha's Rejection
Beta's Bliss
Gamma's Dive
Omega's Folly

The Crystalline Chronicles
The Crystal Eye
The Crystal Archivist
The Crystal Key
The Crystal Heart

The Shifter Brotherhood

Wolf's Blessing

The Tales of Bramoria

The Grimoire of Kings

The Sage and the Phoenix

The Crown of Madness

Standalone

Jonathan's Letter

Lake Arcadia

Watch for more at https://www.blakerwolfe.com.

About the Author

Blake spends most nights with his laptop pulled close, clacking away on the keyboard to get the next great idea written down. Surrounded by piles of notebooks, journals, and a cat of course, he does his best to keep his brain on the task at hand.

Blake has published across multiple genres, but prefers the fantasy realm to all others. He is a beach bum during the summer, a wannabe yogi, and an avid Muppets fan. Seriously.

You can sign up for new releases, giveaways, and freebies on his website.

Read more at https://www.blakerwolfe.com.

Milton Keynes UK
Ingram Content Group UK Ltd.
UKHW040631280723
425958UK00001B/83

9 798223 078647